The Wro... End of T...

by the Hugo-wi... ...ibar

'Of all the envir... ...e
future, Mr Brun... ...nt and
readable. But nev... ...book . . .
Alarming and persuasive.'

Tom Hutchinson, *The Times*

'Mr Brunner has an inexhaustible inventiveness that
makes the book worth reading as a Baedeker of the
fantastic.'

T.A. Shippey, *Times Literary Supplement*

The Wrong End of Time

John Brunner

Methuen Paperbacks
Eyre Methuen

First published in Great Britain
by Eyre Methuen Ltd 1975

Methuen Paperbacks edition first published 1976
Copyright © 1971 by Brunner Fact and Fiction Ltd

Printed for Eyre Methuen Ltd
11 New Fetter Lane, London EC4P 4EE
by Hazell, Watson and Viney Limited Aylesbury, Bucks.

ISBN 0 413 34580 7 (Methuen Paperback)

1

Absolute calm, though not absolute stillness. The sea
shifted lazily against the sandy beach, its motion indexed
not by the white crests of ripples — the water was too oily
for waves to break — but by the pale spots of imperishable
plastic rubbish.

Tangled greenery grew down to within a short distance
of the tide-mark.

Night. The sky was almost clear of cloud. There was no
natural moon, but — as though Phobos and Deimos had
been transported from Mars — two small man-made moons
arced between the stars.

Silence. Only branches rustling and the sound of the
sea.

Less than a mile offshore, a smear of white obtruded
on the glassy water. It could have been due to a partly sub-
merged rock. It was not. It lasted two minutes and disappeared.

Something fractionally blacker than the black ocean
began to approach the land.

A shadow among shadows, Danty Ward crept through
the underbrush. He felt his footing at each step so that he
did not break the night-quiet; nonetheless he managed to
move rather swiftly. He wore a dark jersey and dark pants,
and he had paused by a puddle to smear mud on the high-
lights of his cheekbones and forehead. Gilding the lily in
reverse. He was not following a trodden path, but he was
keeping parallel to and a few yards from a dirt road which
few people travelled. Indeed, hardly anyone came to this

1

stretch of shore at all. It was most inadvisable to try. There were complex alarms and boobytraps, not to mention an electronic fence. Beyond these, hidden among trees and thickets, were highly efficient radar antennae. There were also silos in which were sunk short-range missiles with nuclear warheads of about quarter-megaton capacity. Back near the superway he had passed posters that showed a clenched fist hammering a city into ruins. Underneath captions said: PART OF THE WORLD'S MOST PERFECT DEFENSIVE SYSTEM.

He had taken the precaution of turning everything off.

Somewhere nearby came the scrunching sound of a foot moving in gravel. Danty halted stock-still to *feel* the world, then stealthily made towards the road he had been avoiding. Parting the fronds of a flowering bush, he saw a car on the other side of the track, about twelve feet away. A man leaned against it, his left wrist held close to his face as if he were trying to read his watch in the thin before-dawn light.

With a little nod of satisfaction Danty slipped back into nowhere.

He passed on now towards the beach, coming soon to the point at which the greenery thinned and left only tough dune grasses, courtesy of the Federal Erosion Commission. 'Every man is a piece of the continent, a part of the main; if a clod be washed away by the sea. . .'

Like living on a melting iceberg.

A few yards further on, a boulder stuck its blunt snout up from the sand. Danty looked both ways along the beach, then darted into shelter beside the rock. His back against it, he relaxed, invisible until daylight.

If he was right, though, he would be gone by then.

He stared seaward. Straining his eyes, he discerned something more coherent than a chance assembly of weed or garbage being carried inshore. Matt-dark, but a little shiny because it was wet. Purposively shaped. A man in a

2

survival suit.

Danty allowed himself a grunt of self-approbation, and concentrated on making his relaxation still more complete.

Vassily Sheklov, on the other hand, was tense. He had no qualms about the suit he was wearing — it was a very advanced model, and he would cheerfully have bet on it to carry him through hell-fire. It could not, however, protect him from the oppressive weight of knowledge about his situation which bore down on his skull as though the dome of the night sky were leaning its entire awful burden on his head. He had unwisely allowed the submarine captain to press a last glass of vodka on him, by way of a toast to the success of his mission. The liquor — and his careful yoga exercises — had sustained him during the nerve-racking period while they were inching towards the coast, sometimes within a metre of grounding on the bottom; to duck beneath the sweep-pattern of the radar they knew to be located hereabouts, they had to break surface not more than a kilometre from the beach, where the water was ridiculously shallow for such a big vessel. But now he was out here on his own he was horribly aware of what that slug of alcohol might have done to the speed of his reflexes.

Landing in a spot which was as thick with nuclear missiles as a porcupine's back with spines! He had to keep reminding himself that the paradoxical advice had come from Turpin, who ought to be reliable if anyone was. According to him a reserved area was the safest choice, provided the submarine didn't trigger the automatic firing mechanisms, because Americans were almost superstitious about such places and nobody would be within miles.

Thus far the advice had proved sound. Sheklov noted the fact in the tidy mental card-index of data about Turpin which he was compiling.

His knees touched bottom. He found his footing, and abruptly the buoyancy of his suit converted into weight.

Not a great weight. He stood up with sea around his legs and looked the scene over.

Nothing moved except branches and man-made litter bobbing on the wavelets.

He went up the sand looking for the tide-mark, and found that the full tide, due soon after dawn, would erase all but a few of his footprints. When he gained the protection of the first bushes, he opened his suit and peeled it off. Underneath he wore authentic American leisure clothing, smuggled via Mexico or Canada.

He laid the suit down in a wind-sculpted hollow and hit the destruct switch on its shoulder. Faint smoke drifted up, and the plastic began to deliquesce.

Waiting for the process to go to completion, he used a fronded branch to scuff over the three footprints he had left above the high-water mark. On his return to the suit he found only a puddle of jelly, already beginning to soak into the sand. He shovelled more sand over it with a bit of jetsam and tossed miscellaneous garbage on top of the little pile. Then, with a final glance out to sea to confirm that the submarine had vanished, he headed inland.

Danty rose from his boulder and faded into the undergrowth again. He kept pace, discreetly.

Sheklov found the dirt road easily. The captain had been laudably precise in his navigation. He walked by its edge — carefully, because it had rained here within the past few hours and the ground was soft — until he came within sight of a car: an expensive make which he recognised from his briefing. Waiting beside it, a man raised his arm in hesitant greeting.

Continuing at a neutral pace, Sheklov studied him. He wore a dark jacket and pants, by Russian standards rather old-fashioned. He was about fifty, above medium height, plump-cheeked, paunchy, sweating a little — from nervousness, presumably, because the night was cool. . . Yes,

4

this was Turpin okay. Either that, or someone had gone to a lot of trouble to prepare a duplicate.

Now the man spoke in a wheezy whisper, saying, 'Holtzer?'

Sheklov nodded. For the time being, he was indeed Holtzer.

Turpin let go a gusty sigh and mopped his forehead with a handkerchief. 'Sorry,' he said, the word muffled by its folds. 'The strain of waiting was beginning to get to me. Uh — did you have a good trip?'

'Well, the water was pretty dirty,' Sheklov said, and tensed for the answer. It was conceivable something had gone wrong, at the receiving if not at the delivering end. But Turpin's response was word-perfect.

'Still, the air around here isn't too bad.'

Sheklov let a thought form in his mind.

I made it!

The realisation hit him with almost physical violence, so that he did not immediately react when Turpin opened the car-door and motioned for him to get in. Belatedly he complied, noting the decadent luxury of the vehicle's interior . . . and then the sullen inertia of the door as he closed it.

Armoured, of course. The thing must weigh six or seven tons. And in plain sight next to the radiation-counter: a gun, its muzzle snugly inserted into a socket on the dash, its butt convenient for the driver's right hand.

Well, he was going to have to get used to that kind of thing.

'What about tracks?' he said, thinking of how deeply so much weight could drive tyres into ground as soft as he had just been walking on. Turpin started the car and began to turn it around. It was equipped exclusively with manual controls, naturally. He'd had it dinned into him that over here people liked to gamble with each other's lives on the roads.

'Sonic projectors in the wheel-arches,' Turpin answered.

5

'They homogenise dust and mud. If someone comes by before the next rain he might realise a car has been this way, but he won't have a hope in hell of identifying a tread-pattern. But don't talk until we're out of the reserved area, please. I shall have to use some pretty tricky gadgets to get us through the perimeter alarms. As soon as we hit the superway, though, we can relax.'

The third time he sawed the car back and forth, it was facing in the direction he wanted, and he sent it silently down the track, back to the superway, back to the real America.

When the car had gone, Danty stepped out from the bushes and began to walk unconcernedly in its wake. He was a mile or so from the superway. He would reach it a few minutes before dawn.

He didn't bother to turn the site back on.

2

The mud on Danty's face had dried. Rubbing at it as he walked, he reduced it to a greyish smear. That would have to do until he reached soap and water.

Emerging on to the hard shoulder of the superway between two billboards advertising insurance against juvenile leukaemia and KOENIG'S *INTIMATE* INSULATION, he gazed towards the oncoming traffic. He ignored the long-distance freight-trucks, which had schedules to keep, and concentrated on the last of the night-riders, the lamps of their cars dimming as they headed home for a day's sleep. These were the people who seemed to feel oppressed by the isolation of their continent, even though it was three thousand miles wide, and needed to relieve their tension by simply going, regardless of whether there was any place to go *to*.

It was the third car which stopped: a red and gold Banshee. The dead weight of its armour made it almost nose-dive into the concrete as it responded to its compulsorily excellent brakes. The man at the wheel wore a snughat and tailored fatigues, and also — as he stared at Danty — an expression of surprise.

Not at what he saw. Danty was ordinary enough to look at, apart from the mud on his face: young, thin, mid-brown complexion, sharp chin, dark eyes above which his brows formed a shallow V. But at the notion of stopping for him in a state where hitch-hiking had been illegal for decades.

Before he could recover his presence of mind, however, Danty had sauntered over and leaned on his door. Rashly,

7

the man was driving with its window open.

'Going to Lakonia?' he inquired.

'Uh. . .' The driver licked his lips, hand hovering close to his dashboard gun. 'Now look here! I didn't stop to give you a ride! I —'

And broke off in consternation. The question had just occurred to him: *Then why in hell did I stop?*

He could see no other reason than Danty. Who went on looking at him levelly.

'Ah, shit,' the driver said at last. 'Okay, get in. Yes, I am heading for Lakonia.'

'Thanks,' Danty said, and went around to the passenger's door.

Before his unwelcome companion had fastened his safety-harness, the driver stamped on the accelerator and shot back into the centre of the road, watching his mirror anxiously — not so much for following cars, as for a patrolman who might have witnessed that entirely unlawful pickup. The speedo needle reached the limit mark and stopped climbing; nonetheless their speed increased perceptibly afterwards. Danty concealed a grin. Another reason for the driver to feel worried. Plainly he'd eased the control on the governor. Everybody did that, but you were still liable to arrest if you were caught.

Relaxing after a mile or two without incident, the driver reached for the cigarette dispenser.

'Want one?' he asked reluctantly.

'Thanks.' Danty shook his head. 'Don't use them.'

The driver took his, ready-lit, and sucked on it twice before speaking again, this time with the petty bravado of a man defying the law and trying not to let the fact bother him.

'Now don't you get the idea I go around the country free-lifting all the time!'

'Of course not,' Danty said equably.

'So you'd better be a friend of mine, hm? Just in case. My name's Rollins, George Rollins. What's yours and

8

where are you from?'

'Danty. And it says Cowville in my redbook.'

Rollins betrayed obvious relief. Cowville was right next door to Lakonia; in fact it was the nucleus from which Lakonia had spread, like a stump of wild-rose root with a gorgeous over-blown double floribunda grafted on it. Taking a man back to his home city wasn't too bad. Danty let the idea curdle.

Then he added mildly, 'But mostly I'm from all over.'

'You make a habit of travelling this way?' Rollins curled his lip. It was probably in his mind to add: *Because if you do, you must be a lousy reb! Everybody knows they shave and cut their hair nowadays!*

'No, this is kind of a special case.'

'Glad to hear it!' Rollins snapped, and fell silent. After a moment he reached for the radio buttons and snapped on an early morning music programme. Soothed by the sound of the current chart-toppers, the Male Organs, Danty dozed.

He awoke to a prod in his ribs and the sound of the gas-gauge emitting a penetrating hum.

'Got to pull in for gas,' Rollins told him unnecessarily. 'Now you watch how you act, hear? Don't want some radiated gas-attendant to turn me in for free-lifting!'

Danty touched the gritty mud on his face. He said, 'Well, then I can get to a washroom and clean up.'

'You do that! And watch yourself!' Rollins ordered.

His imitation bravado leaked away as the car slowed. His lips moved as though he were rehearsing what he would say when they stopped.

He was. Therefore it came out smoothly enough. 'Fifty, please!' he called to the attendant in his overhead booth, watching the forecourt through armour-glass with his hands poised above the triggers for his guns.

'Fifty it is,' the man answered, and began to haul on his waldoes. Angled, a fuel-pipe launched down from its high hook and sought the car's filler like a blind snake.

So far, so good. As Danty left his seat, Rollins breathed easier. Hell, was anyone — even a gas-attendant, in a trade which encouraged paranoia — going to turn him in for a little free-lifting? Of course not!

And then his stomach filled with ice-cubes. There was a cop rolling into the gas-station, masked and armoured, like a mere extension of the single-seat racer which he rode.

Patrolman Clough yawned hugely as he dismounted. That was a slow job, involving a thorough survey of the vicinity, then the folding back of four light-alloy bullet deflectors. But finally he freed himself, stood upright, and stretched and yawned again. The quick dash of midnight had worn off, and he was having to pull in more and more often to rest up. The endless concentration tired the brain. Police racers had no governors on them, only a red line at the hundred-fifty mark which the rider was forbidden to exceed except in emergency. Something to boast about in company — 'they don't turn loose any but the picked best on the superway without a governor' — but on the job, not so much fun.

Only one car in the station. Banshee. Cheapjack make. Slick lines, sure, but inside — well, built-in obsolescence, of course. Trouble being they sometimes guessed wrong, the obsolescence progressed too quickly, and then he or someone was picking bits of people out of the wreckage.

Not this one, though. A last-month's model, red and gold.

Driver sort of nervy. . . Wonder if he's disconnected his governor. Sort of thing the guy who buys a Banshee might do. Easy to short the governor circuits on one of these. Not a bad idea to have him lift the hood, take a quick squint.

He snapped back the visor of his helmet and strode towards the car.

10

Rollins rubbed sweaty palms inconspicuously on the sides of his thighs. 'Morning, officer!' he exclaimed, and damned his voice for skating up towards the treble.

The patrolman gave a neutral nod. Rollins told himself he couldn't possibly have seen the disreputable passenger, and whatever was bothering him with luck he'd guess wrong and be away before Danty emerged from the washroom. In fact it might be a good idea to get back on the road without Danty, if he could. What in the world could have possessed him to stop for a free-lifter? And a reb at that, more than likely!

The gas-pipe withdrew to its hook. A cash-drawer shot out of the side of the pump within easy reach of him. But he was so intent on the patrolman that at first he didn't notice, and the attendant had to parp on his hooter.

Damnation. Now the pig will know I'm rattled. He fumbled a credit-card from his pocket and laid it in the tray. The patrolman followed every move, and when the drawer had clicked shut he said, 'Mind lifting your hood, mister?'

'Uh. . .' Well, there was no help for it. He flipped the release and the hood ascended three feet on lazy-tongs mountings, sighing. *Look, officer, I have a clean licence ten years old, everyone eases the governor control a bit, it's not as though I'd been in an accident. . .*

But the patrolman only glanced at the engine, nodded, and made to turn away. Rollins exhaled gratefully.

Must have thought the governor was cut out completely. Who but a damned fool — ?

And Danty reappeared.

He'd washed, and wiped the stubble of beard from his chin with Depilide, but even so he didn't match a brand-new Banshee. And here he was opening the passenger door. You could almost hear the tumblers clicking in the pig's head, like a fruit machine.

'Hah!' he said after a tense pause. 'Let's see your redbook, you!'

Danty shrugged, unzipped his hip-pocket, and held out

11

his red-covered identity papers. The silence stretched as the patrolman seemed to be reading every single word. Finally Rollins could bear it no longer.

'Is something wrong, officer?'

The cop didn't glance up. He said, 'Friend of yours, mister?'

'Sure. Of course he is!'

'Tell me more.' The machine-like helmet still bent over the redbook.

'Uh. . .' Rollins's mind raced. 'Why, Danty's from Cowville. Close to where I live. We just been night-riding a bit, that's all.'

Though if he asks what this radiated reb's other name is. . .!

The patrolman slapped shut and returned the redbook. 'Okay,' was all he said, but under his voice, clear as shouting, he was adding: *So, a couple fruits most likely. I should arrest that kind on suspicion? I'd be at it all day. Anyway, they'd jump bail and head for a state where it's allowed.*

Frantically Rollins started the engine again, eager to get away from here.

'Your credit card,' Danty said, and pointed. Rollins snarled, snatched it from the cash-drawer, and trod on the gas. Danty was amused to see that he must have worked out what the pig was thinking. He was blushing scarlet clear down to his collar.

Behind them, Patrolman Clough made a routine entry in his tape-recording log. But, two or three minutes later, as he was emerging from the men's room, a car howled past at far above the legal limit, and he scrambled back on his racer and took out after it, yelling for assistance on his radio. In the excitement of the chase he clean forgot about Danty and Rollins.

12

3

Turpin was plainly ill at ease and could not make up his mind how to open a conversation. For the time being that suited Sheklov. He wanted to get the feel of America, hammering home on the automatic level what he had learned on the conscious. Already he had noticed a contradiction. From the radio which Turpin had switched on, as though by reflex, music was emanating of a kind which he himself had barely encountered since his teens, when his generation still thought it 'progressive' and 'liberal' to imitate the example of Western rock-groups. The sound was imbued with curious nostalgia. Then, between items, an announcer resolved the paradox by saying that the programme was aimed at the eternally youthful and proceeding to advertise a skin-food.

For men, as well as women. He sniffed. Yes, he wasn't mistaken; Turpin was heavily perfumed with something which hadn't been detectable in the open air, but had built up in the closed metal box of the car, despite the conditioning, until it was overpowering. He thought of asking for a window to be opened, but changed his mind. He was going to have to adjust.

To things like this superway, for instance. Back home, the roads he knew were typically two or at most three lanes wide, laid with geometrical exactitude across the landscape, carrying far more trucks and hundred-passenger buses than private cars, and had control cables laid under the surface so that no mere human being should be called on to avert an accident at 200 k.p.h.

But roads weren't really important. You could use less

13

land and shift more people with a hovertrain riding concrete pylons, or for long distances you would fly.

When this road, with its opulent curves, came to a rise in the ground, its builders had contrived to give the impression that it eased itself up to let the hill pass beneath. Elegant, certainly. Yet so wasteful! Eight lanes in each direction, not because there was so much traffic, only because that much margin must be allowed for human error.

Thinking of speed. . . He repressed a start as he looked at the speedometer. Oh, yes. Not k.p.h., but m.p.h.; the Americans had resolutely clung to their antiquated feet, yards and miles, just as they had clung to Fahrenheit when the rest of the world abandoned it. Even so, he hoped that Turpin was a reasonably competent driver. He himself had never attempted to guide a land-vehicle at such velocity.

Now, finally, Turpin was addressing him: 'Cigarette?'

'Please.' It would be interesting to try American tobacco. But he found it hot, dry, and lacking in aroma.

Ahead, a lighted beacon warned traffic to merge into the left lanes, and shortly, as the car slowed, he saw something that confirmed his worst fears: a wreck involving two trucks and a private car around which a gang of black men were busy with chains, jacks and cutting-torches. On the centre divide an ambulance-crew waited anxiously to be offered a cargo.

When was someone last killed on the roads, Back There?

He watched Turpin covertly as they passed the spot, and read no emotion whatever on his face.

Well, to sustain his pretence for so long, obviously he must have had to repress his natural reactions. . .

Yet Sheklov found the explanation too glib to be convincing.

Then, a little further on, they encountered another gang of workmen, also black, being issued with tools from

14

a truck on the hard-shoulder. Some of them were setting up more beacons. That was a phenomenon Sheklov had been briefed about: a 'working welfare' project. Obviously they were here to repair the road; equally obviously, the road didn't need repairing. But it conformed to the American ideal: you don't work, you don't eat.

He felt a surge of pride as he reflected on the superior efficiency of a planned economy. Then, sternly, he dismissed the thought. The system must work, otherwise human beings could not tolerate it. It was not for him to say that it oughtn't to work. Enclosed, isolated, offensively conceited, the Americans were still human, and what they did among themselves was *ipso facto* to be respected as part of the vast repertoire of human potential.

Drawing a deep breath, he closed his eyes for a moment. Words formed in memory; they said, 'O Dhananjaya, abandoning attachment and regarding success and failure alike, be steadfast in Yoga and perform thy duties.'

And his duty at present was to be Donald Paton Holtzer, who had never heard of the Blessed Lord's Song.

There was considerable traffic on the move. He saw hundreds of cars, mostly as they were left behind, because Turpin had clearance for the fastest lanes, but two or three times howling monsters tore past them illegally on the inside, and once they were overtaken by a patrolman on a racer with his siren howling like a soul in torment.

The roads, while still in usable condition, were being torn up and re-made. So too the cars were destined for a short, short life. Everything about this silent limousine of Turpin's was ultra-modern, including its schedule of obsolescence. Approximately six months old, it was already as close to the scrapyard as to the factory.

And from the scrapyard its elements would go to the factory again.

Talk about taking in each other's washing. . . But he slapped that down in his mind, too.

Now and then they passed in sight of enormous housing developments, and Sheklov also studied these carefully. Apartments stacked in towering blocks. Gardens around them, or parks. Trees in neat lines, force-grown with para-gibberellins. He found them attractive, but somehow flawed — perhaps by the way they resembled one another, as though they had been mass-produced complete with occupants. They were becoming shabby. His briefings had included a thorough conspectus of the cycle of American fads and fashions, and he was able to date them as having been built about twenty-five years ago — just about the time, indeed, that Turpin was planted in the States.

Reminded of his companion, he turned his head. Turpin's eyes were on him.

'You're very quiet,' Sheklov said.

Turpin gave a plump-jowled grin. 'I figured you'd start talking in your own good time. Make the most of this ride, though. I do have a bug-free room at home, of course, but this car is even safer. And we're coming pretty close to Lakonia now.'

He seemed to have recovered completely from his earlier nervousness.

'Frankly,' Sheklov said, 'I was expecting you to ask what brought me here. I gather you weren't informed of the details.' He spoke easily in the language he had practised non-stop during his briefing period.

'I didn't question the decision,' Turpin said stiffly. 'After all, I've been thoroughly absorbed by now, and your people —' He bit something back.

'Go on,' Sheklov encouraged.

'All right, I'll have to get around to it sooner or later. Your people don't seem to set much store by me nowadays.'

Sheklov displayed genuine surprise. 'I don't know where you got that impression! I've always heard that your complete assimilation has made you the most valuable single agent we've ever had here. Why else would

16

they have called on you to cushion my arrival?'

Turpin didn't answer, but pressed his lips together in a thin line. Sheklov could gloss that expression easily enough. *Because you'd have been told I was good, to bolster your own confidence; or because I'm to be eliminated and you're to replace me; or because you're expendable yourself, and meant to bring about our joint downfall; or because I'm suspect and you've been assigned to investigate me. . .*

Turpin sighed. 'Oh, what's the point of worrying? I do as I'm told, that's all. I laid on exactly the cover for you that was requested — you're Canadian, timber-salesman, been down here sounding out a new pulp contract, recommended to Energetics General by your parent firm, looking for a supplier of plastic glue for bonding chipboard, staying with me at Lakonia because we're very eager to close that deal. Which is true; we're short of foreign currency, as you know. There's a bag in the trunk for you, with clothes, ticket-stubs, hotel bills, a raft of genuine material. Anyway, the fact that I speak for you will protect you from security.'

That sounded too pat. Sheklov was about to voice a question, when Turpin added, 'And for extra insurance I'll have you photographed with Prexy.'

He tossed that off casually also, but if it was a promise he could keep, Sheklov felt, he was entitled to be proud of his record. They had told him over and over how well-established Turpin was, and though he reserved the right to doubt it until he saw it happen he was prepared to believe that Turpin could indeed invoke the President to reinforce his cover.

'You brought up the purpose of your visit,' Turpin went on. 'I imagine it's to check me out. Don't think I'll be offended if you tell me.'

There was overt bitterness in his tone. Sheklov saw in that a reason why the people Back There might have downgraded this man in their minds. But if they had none of them had let slip the slightest suggestion of the fact.

'It's nothing to do with you at all,' he grunted. 'We've run into a problem we can't solve. We're at our wits' end. And since we've looked everywhere else for ideas, we're finally being driven to look for some over here.'

He wondered if his own scepticism showed in his voice. He was thinking: *Pluto! Hell! Half the people in this country probably never heard of it, and the rest must be old enough to remember Disney's dog.*

Turpin took a fresh cigarette. 'Hah! It must be quite a problem, then. Explain! I want to know what's so important that I have to risk everything I've built up in twenty-five years.'

Sheklov marshalled his words carefully. He'd rehearsed this introductory exposition many times, of course. He said, 'As a senior vice-president of Energetics General, you must know as much as any one man about the defence system of this continent. Right?'

'Why not? We designed most of it. We still contract for its servicing. And have I ever failed to notify your people of our newest developments?'

'No, you haven't,' Sheklov said fervently, and felt a shiver go down his spine. In a sense, the fact that Earth had not long ago dissolved into a nuclear holocaust was due to this man at his side. It was awe-inspiring to reflect on that.

'So tell me,' he continued when he had recovered from his brief access to wonder, 'what would happen if — say — New York were wiped off the map by a total-conversion reaction.'

'A — *what?*' Turpin jerked in his seat. Ash fell from his cigarette to his thigh. He brushed at it, and missed.

'Total-conversion, I said. Well?'

'Well. Uh. . .' Turpin licked his lips. 'Well, it would depend on whether anything had been detected coming down from orbit.'

'Something would have.'

'Well, then. Uh. . . Well, everything in the sky not accounted for by the flight-plan at Aerospace HQ would be taken out by ground missiles. That's automatic. Then the orbital hardware would be activated, and you'd lose the tovs.'

'Tobs?'

'*Tovs.* Didn't they give you that? Careless! Short for *tovarich*. That's what we call your manned satellites.'

You: we. Force of habit, probably. Camouflage. But Sheklov found himself wondering how deep the camouflage went in Turpin's mind after a quarter of a century.

'Is there a lot of orbital hardware?'

'Enough,' Turpin said, and gave a thin smile. 'Sorry, but you might let slip something you're not supposed to know.'

Sheklov allowed him the petty victory. He said, 'And then?'

'Within about two minutes, the Nightsticks would be homing on their targets. They're solid-fuelled inertial-guided missiles with —'

'Yes, we know about those. Thanks to you.'

He said it deliberately, to determine how much the reminder would affect Turpin. The answer was — severely. He stuttered for several seconds.

'Anyway!' he pursued. 'Within eight minutes and thirty seconds twelve thousand megatons would go down on East Bloc territory. And if there were another —'

Sheklov held up his hand. 'The world's most perfect defensive system. Yes. We've taken great care for many years to avoid tripping this country's deadly burglar alarms, but they still exist, which means that people must think they're still necessary.'

'We're doing our best to cure that.' Turpin said with a hint of anxiety. 'Though naturally in my position I daren't —'

'Daren't do anything that might cast suspicion on your cover,' Sheklov cut in. 'Sure, we understand just how

19

tough security can be over here. But what's your response to the news that some American city may well be converted into raw energy in the near future?'

A haunted expression came and went on Turpin's face, as though for the first time in years he was reviewing the implications of setting off twelve thousand megatons of nuclear explosive. He said, 'You mean the Chinese have —'

'Chinese, hell. The Chinese don't have a total-conversion reaction! Nobody has it, down here.'

Understanding began to turn Turpin's cheeks to grey.

'Yes,' Sheklov said with a nod. 'Out near Pluto we've met — someone else.'

4

Who?

Well, one thing — so Sheklov had been told — was definite. They couldn't be from this part of the galaxy, or even from this part of the cosmos. Because their ship sparkled. Even at the orbit of Pluto it was continually being touched by dust particles. On contact, they vanished into energy. Which demonstrated that the vessel, and hence by logic the system where it originated, must be contraterrene.

The aliens didn't seem to mind. Apparently they could take care of that problem. They could take care of the human race just as easily, if they chose.

Or, more precisely: they could arrange for the human race to take care of itself.

'They're far ahead of us,' Sheklov said when Turpin's grey face had started back towards its normal colour. 'We're afraid of them. So far we haven't managed to communicate anything to them, although we've been trying for more than three years. Somehow or other we *must* establish rapport, because if we can't convince them we're fit to get along with they're not only able but apparently willing to set us back a thousand years. In the way I suggested — by turning an American city into energy.'

'If you can't communicate with them, how do you know?' Turpin snapped.

'The problem is strictly one-sided. They proved that they know a great deal about us, by projecting pictures in a gas-cloud floating in space. The experts say they must have generated localised artificial gravity-fields to create their images, then excited them to radiate in appropriate colours. We aren't within centuries of such techniques.'

Contraterrene. . . Implying that anything they launched at Earth would boil its entire mass into energy — and what hope was there of intercepting the missiles of a species which must be more advanced by millennia than mankind? And they knew about 'the world's most perfect defensive system'. Inasmuch as any clear information could be deduced from the images they projected in their gas-clouds — a series of still pictures, with incredibly fine detail — they were having second thoughts about opening formal relations with mankind. One could guess that they didn't approve of a race which was capable of destroying its own members.

So now problems which had gone unsolved for generations *had* to be solved. There was no way of predicting when the aliens' patience might run out. When it did, they could — and maybe would — pitch the human race back to the caves. There had been one final picture which rankled in Sheklov's memory; naturally, he had studied photographs of them all. And that one showed a dirty, mis-shapen, but recognisable man, wrapped in a raw animal-hide, waving a stone axe. . .

He who is the same to friend and foe, and also in honour and dishonour, the same in heat and cold, pleasure and pain, free from all attachment. . .

With overtones: 'who doesn't give a damn!' But that was an impossible ideal. Sheklov checked the thought, because Turpin was asking him another question.

'So you think someone here might be able to communicate with the aliens? But without explaining the real reason, I couldn't get funds for research into the problem, and —'

'You misunderstand me,' Sheklov interrupted. 'If the solution were technical, we'd have licked it by now. What we want is. . . I guess you'd say a new attitude of mind.'

Turpin shook his head, confused. 'Well, we do have

22

some pretty competent psychologists on the payroll.'

A picture arose in Sheklov's memory: old Bratcheslav-sky, cross-legged on a bare floor, fingers yellow to the second knuckle with cigarette-stains, saying, 'Do this without preconceptions, Vassily. Ask the questions when you get there.' Behind him, through the window, the white towers of Alma-Ata turned to grey by winter overcast.

Sheklov said, 'One thing I was told I should ask you as soon as I arrived. What's a "reb"?'

'Reb?' Turpin echoed in an astonished tone. 'Why — why, a reb is a good-for-nothing, a dropout, a parasite. Someone who refuses to work and lives by scrounging. They come in two sexes: "johnnyreb" for a boy, "jenny-reb" for a girl. Why?'

'You mean they're beggars?' Sheklov groped.

'I guess so. Most of them don't even have the get-up-and-go to turn thief. You see them all the time on the Cowville shore of New Lake; there's some sort of colony over there. Just sitting! Just staring at the water and the clouds.'

'Meditating?' Sheklov suggested.

'They use the word for an excuse. I don't believe it.'

He seemed to feel very strongly about rebs, Sheklov noted. He pondered a while, then murmured, 'A kind of saddhu?'

'What?'

'Saddhu. An Indian holy man. Lives by begging.'

'Nothing holy about a reb!' Turpin rasped. And, suddenly conscious of the ferocity of his tone, added, 'What in the world made you ask about rebs?'

'Curiosity, that's all,' Sheklov lied. 'Of course back home we don't have people like that.'

Turpin gave a satisfied nod. That, Sheklov deduced, must be one of the things that was still sustaining him after a quarter-century: the belief that what most offended him in the society of his adopted country was elsewhere unknown. The grass is always greener — as it were.

23

Whereas I. . .

Looking down as the superway crossed a tall viaduct, he spotted another of the isolated townships which it by-passed: this one brand-new, sparkling in the morning sun, alive with cars like multi-coloured maggots as the bread-winners of the community left for work. It raced rear-ward, dwindled, was followed by another: lush, luxurious — but mass-produced, people and all.

Suddenly uncaged in his mind, the doubts and disbe-liefs he had dutifully tried to conquer came striding back with echoing, lead-heavy steps.

There is no wisdom for the unsteady and there is no meditation for the unsteady and for the unmeditative there is no peace. How can there be any happiness for those without peace?

Are all human beings mentally deformed? Why else should they think in negatives all the time? Health is more than the absence of overt sickness, sanity more than the absence of dangerous psychosis. Peace too must be more than the absence of a shooting war. Peace must be. . .

No use. He could sense it, recognise it as possible. But he could not make it real in his mind. He had seen people who were apparently at peace — there was the kicker — but he had never accomplished it himself.

Anyway, if you do reach that unscalable pinnacle, what about the rest of the world?

He almost cried aloud, in anguish; he almost asked, *How long before the world is cured of finding patchwork solutions to single problems — solutions that generate problems in their turn? It's bad enough Back There, but here. . .!*

Men assembling in the cold morning light to tear up a road with pick and shovel so it could be re-laid by a machine!

America, of all countries, he mourned silently. *Why did they send me to America?*

When he was young he had spent three years in the

24

India which had ultimately chosen to preserve its heritage, rather than accept aid conditional upon alliance with one of the great power-blocs. There, many people were sick, most were ill-fed and ill-housed.

And some were happy.

How long before we start looking for a way of life in which problems don't matter?

Turpin was still making wouldbe-helpful suggestions, proposing to invoke the resources of his company, its psychologists, its computers, its enormous data-banks. It seemed he had completely missed the point.

Not that Sheklov felt he understood it properly himself.

Listening, he came to suspect that Turpin was simply uttering polite noises. News of something 'out near Pluto' — even if it could distort the totality of human experience, eastern and western — had no concrete referents for him. A generation of isolation, half-voluntary, half-enforced, had coloured the thinking of his adopted countrymen, of whom he was so contemptuous; inevitably, though, in order to protect himself among them, he had had to let his own thinking be conditioned by their example.

In which case. . .

As a loyal agent, Sheklov found the conclusion he was being driven to repugnant. Yet he had to face it. He was compelled to wonder whether those who had sent him here genuinely believed they were dispatching him on the trail of a clue, or whether they had merely lapsed into the pattern of the old days, when America was the wealthy rival, to be first emulated, then surpassed.

But that attitude was obsolete. The paths of the two blocs had diverged a long way now.

Though, of course, since they were both branches of the same species, the people who lived under the aegis of these supposedly irreconcilliable systems coincided in surprising ways. If he were to go into one of those handsome housing developments overlooked by the superway, would

he not find, as he would Back There, people who contrived casually to mention their courage in moving to a
building which wasn't blast-proof? And kept a year's sup-
ply of food in the freezer anyway?

Of course I would.

They would take pains to impress him with their loyal-
ty, their right thinking; they would have the proper photographs and flags on display. Small matter if they were
afraid of some impersonal, august, omniscient Security
Force, rather than of the cold consensus of their neighbours — the effect was essentially the same. They would
strive to be dedicated pillars of their community, set on
raising their children to follow in their footsteps, endless-
ly quarrelling with them when they scoffed or asked un-
answerable questions.

But he had seen a man under a tree: thin, wearing only
a loincloth, one eye filmed with a cataract, who spent the
day in ecstatic enjoyment of the sun's heat on his skin,
and at nightfall fumbled in the bowl before him and ate
what he found. There was always something in the bowl.

After that he had to be Donald Holtzer again, and Holtzer was not troubled by such thoughts.

5

Almost within sight of Lakonia, the Banshee caught up with a shower of rain, quite likely the same one which had provided Danty with that puddle where he had found mud for his face. At the first drops the wipers churred into action and the windows attempted to close. But Danty, lost in thought, was sitting with his elbow on the passenger door, and the automatics uttered a whine of complaint.

Rollins snapped at him. With a murmured apology he moved his arm. The glass socketed home in the spongy seal around the roof, and Rollins breathed an audible sigh of relief.

'You wear lead, hm?' Danty suggested, and gave a pointed scowl at the counter on the dash next to the gun. Its needle was well down in the white sector. By reflex Rollins also glanced at it, and then flushed, indicating the road ahead slick with wet as far as could be seen.

'You want to get soaked, get out and walk!'

He looked and sounded as though he fully expected the counter to zoom into the red any moment.

Danty shrugged? So it wasn't rational to be that afraid of rain; there was Sr-90 and C-14 in everything you ate and drank, and unless you wore lead underwear you were constantly at risk from the long-life gamma-emitters like Cs-137. But, as he reminded himself wryly, Rollins was far from the only person in the world who did irrational things.

Maybe he did wear Koenig's, at that. He wasn't apt to admit it to a stranger, though.

Then the superway rounded the shoulder of a hill, and

he caught his breath. Still in bright sunlight, by a freak of the rainstorm's course, there was Lakonia laid out before them.

Symptom of a terrible disease, like the 'hectic flush' of tuberculosis, conveying the illusion of vigorous health, or like the frenzied mental brilliance of terminal syphilis? Some authorities regarded it that way. They claimed that Lakonia was an ersatz, a surrogate; this city built around an artificial sea, they said, was a palliative to dull the guilt suffered by those who had poisoned first the Great Lakes, then the rivers, and ultimately the inshore waters of the oceans past the point at which a man could swim in them.

Yet in its way — and seeing it now Danty was the last person who could have denied it — it was a place of mad magnificence, a rival to the Pyramids and Babylon.

Its towers rose, white, purple, green and gold, to meet the sun: towers like stalactites, like poplar trees; towers like stacks of coins, each offset on the one below; towers like spun sugar-candy, glittering, and towers like frozen waterspouts. High delicate bridges linked them here and there, slung on ropes of spun carbon-fibres seeming weak and thin as spider's webs yet capable of carrying cars nose to tail in both directions, and the thicker, ivory-coloured single rail of the hoverline swerved and swooped from one to the next. And all these pinnacles admired their reflections in pure crystal water — moats around the towers' roots, canals planned to a scale beside which Venice paled.

In any case, Venice had collapsed.

Uniting all these waterways, the New Lake: man-made, spanning eight miles shore to shore, which gave Lakonia the first syllable of its name.

It was early yet, and there was no way of telling whether the nearby rain might not drift in that direction, but the bright mirror of water was alive — with swimmers,

with sail-boats, with powered launches towing water-skiers
and man-carrying kites. At least, the nearside of the lake
was swarming with them. Some mile, or mile and a half,
from the shore, they seemed by tacit consent to turn back,
to face again towards the high lovely towers and the artificial beach of white imported sand. It was as though on
the further shore there was something they were afraid to
approach. Yet, looking in that direction, an uninstructed
stranger would have seen nothing more foreboding than a
stand of tall dark trees, force-grown redwoods two hundred feet high, above which curled a faint wreath of
smoke.

'You live in Lakonia?' Danty asked as the road slanted
down.

'Yes,' Rollins snapped, more of his attention on his driving now than at any time since Danty stopped him. Here
the traffic was thickening like milk soured by lemon-juice.
'And you don't. So where do you want to be put off?'

'Any hoverhalt will do.'

'Sure you don't want to be run all the way home?' Rollins countered sarcastically. 'If you have a home, that is.'

'I get by,' Danty said.

Rollins spotted a vacant parking bay and pulled over.
The car, stopped, rocking. Ahead was a hoverhalt sign, a
blue illuminated arrow pointing up.

'Thanks,' Danty murmured, opening the door. Rollins
didn't answer. In another few seconds he was lost to sight
in the river of traffic and Danty was dropping coins in the
turnstile of the hoverhalt.

Five minutes, and the luxury and beauty of Lakonia
lay behind him. He was beyond the forced redwoods and
in the shadow — for a few seconds, literally, because it
was as tall as the underlying rock would bear and loomed
far above the forty-foot level of the hoverline — of the
Energetics General Building, four city blocks by five.

In the centre of Cowville, that huge squat bulk brooded like a queen-bee in her hive. It was the headquarters of the biggest single employer in the country, except government, and of course without government it could not survive. Sometimes Danty thought of it as a temple, the fane of the priests who served the god Defence.

Cowville was old. Some said it was the oldest city in the state. The insertion of that hulking building into its centre had deformed it in a curious fashion, like the pressure of a wedge being hammered home in a block of wood. People — and the buildings they lived and worked in — seemed not so much to cluster around this focus of vast wealth, as to have been compressed by it, like garbage compacted for disposal. They were prevented from expanding outside the original city limits by strictly-enforced ordinances, because nothing must interfere with the beautiful setting of Lakonia. Not all of them had come to seek work, or to take advantage of the money flowing freely around Energetics General at a time when half the states of the Union were depressed; some had come merely in order to live close to Lakonia, for the privilege of walking to the lakeshore and staring at its towers, focus of indescribable ambitions which they would never fulfil.

Even so there was little resentment of its existence. Lakonia had salvaged a beloved scrap of the American dream. At a time when people were losing faith in their older god, Business, because it had fouled the air and ruined the countryside and made the rivers stink, one corporation had created a new and lovely lake, whose water was purer than a mountain creek.

After that, over ten years, came the city: the most desirable place to live on the continent.

Meantime they shut away, behind trees, the original city of Cowville, and — apart from what unavoidable maintenance was called for to keep it habitable — let it rot. They were content to say, 'You don't grow a rose without manure.'

Yet, like the nearly-but-not-quite flavour of hydroponic food, life in Lakonia lacked something. A spice. A savour. 'I remember it from the old days,' people claimed — then when challenged to describe it, confessed they couldn't. 'Nonetheless,' they maintained stoutly, 'it was real! It can't have vanished completely.'

Therefore, now and then, they set off in search of it, and for want of anywhere better to start looking they came to Cowville, to the littered streets and the stores crammed with over-priced knick-knacks and the pre-Lakonia apartment blocks which had been sub-divided and sub-divided again. It was hard to find living-space in Cowville now. One could foresee an end like the ancient Chinese system of land-tenure, the ancestral holding split up among successive generations until a family was compelled to share a broom-closet.

If they looked in the wrong places they got robbed, or raped, or slashed with a bottle in a bar. But if they were lucky, or someone had given them the right advice beforehand, they learned to recognise landmarks — signposts, clues. A message on a wall, chalked up at midnight, at four a.m. washed away by rain. In a store, a handwritten notice: MEETING, followed by a date, a time, an address. In the window of an apartment, a cheap printed card: THINGS FOUND. Nature of the things not specified. TRACING AGENTS. PROBLEMS SERVICE. CASES UNDERTAKEN.

You could follow these signs if you chose. They led to another city altogether. They led to the city Danty lived in.

He left the hovercar at a halt on the roof of one of the city's oldest surviving buildings, a good sixty years old. It seemed like a logical idea, when they extended the line around the lake, to use existing roofs for halts, but they had had to straitjacket the building with concrete beams when the recurrent vibration threatened to shake it down. Now the beams served a double purpose, acting also as

31

supports for an exterior staircase and for landings on three sides of the building. The interior stairways and the elevator shaft had been turned into shower-rooms and kitchenettes. There had been two apartments on the top floor of this building; now there were eight, entered by doors which had been regular windows.

In the remaining window of the apartment nearest the stairs, dimly legible through the wire-reinforced glass, a card said simply CONSULTATIONS. It was into this one that Danty let himself, with a key which he wore on a steel chain around his neck. It was a precious key; there were only two like it. It was risky to use a stock type of lock in modern Cowville, because so many people had complete collections of the American Lock and Vault Corporation's range. If you could afford it, you had one hand-made.

The apartment trembled a little as the hovercar he'd arrived on accelerated towards its next destination.

'Magda!' Danty called as he shut the door. There was no answer. He hadn't really expected one, unless she was in the toilet.

The apartment consisted of one large room, along two walls of which couches that doubled as divans had been built in, plus an alcove off with a curtain, a shower-cabinet, and a kitchen made of fire-proof board. As always, it was untidy, with a dozen books lying around open, a stack of sheets torn from a notepad in the middle of the one large low table. He glanced at the latter to make sure none bore a message for him, but they were covered in indecipherable technicalities.

He swore under his breath. Of course, she did have many other calls on her time, but you'd have thought that today. . .

His resentment died. Maybe it was better this way. Maybe he needed a chance to think over what he had done. Until he was in sight of Lakonia, he'd been able to mute knowledge of his own actions in his mind, making them distant and dreamlike. Now they were throbbing and pounding in his memory.

More to distract himself than because he was hungry, he brought a soyburger and a carton of milk out of the freeze, switched on the TV and sat down to eat in front of it. He caught the tail-end of the weather forecast, and then followed the day's counts: pollen, RA — high beta, low gamma — KC's, Known Carcinogens, SO_2 and the rest. But he wasn't paying attention. He was thinking about the man from the sea.

Images came to his mind; he pictured the disturbance the stranger would cause, like a small, very hard pebble dropped into a loose-journalled complex of machinery. Slack would be taken up here and there in its bearings. Bit by bit it would become possible to deduce who he was, why he had come, what he hoped to achieve.

And then, perhaps, something would have to be done.

'Do thou therefore perform right and obligatory actions,' he quoted to himself under his breath, 'for action is superior to inaction.'

With a sudden violent gesture he thrust away his plate. He linked his brown thin fingers together so tightly the knuckles paled. His teeth threatened to chatter, so that he had to knot his jaw-muscles to hold them still.

Magda! For pity's sake hurry back!
I'm scared!

6

Lora Turpin had had all she could take, and said so to her mother. Her mother, with her usual infuriating white satin calmness — out of a bottle with 'White Satin' on the label — called her a misbegotten moron and suggested that radiation must have affected the ovum from which she was conceived. That finished the discussion. Theatrically Lora stormed out of the room, out of the apartment, out of the building, and into a hovercar going anywhere.

If it had been night, she would have driven; there were five cars in the basement garage she could get the keys for. But she hated sawing through slow day-time traffic, and what was more she was forbidden to ride the hoverline, which was why she did it when she was in a bad temper.

This time it didn't lead to the anticipated result. Naturally, because she was very pretty, several men leered at her, but they were all reeky ancients, at least forty, and the only hand which did try stroking her bare waist belonged to a fat mannish woman who got off at the second halt. It was around then that she realised, as the redwood trees loomed ahead, that this car was heading in the wrong direction. She'd meant to get off at a halt by one of the yacht-pools and pick up a boy with a boat. She hadn't had a boy for over a week.

Almost, she made to leave the car. But she changed her mind. What the hell? She'd never ridden a Cowville line to the end.

Curious, she watched the squalid city slide beneath, and then around, as the line approached the monstrous mausoleum of Energetics General, and then beneath again: an area of lower buildings, harking vainly back to the foundation of the city, to the pioneering image of the original cow-town. A mobile illuminated figure shamelessly copied from 'Vegas Vic' beckoned customers to a block crowded with twenty-four-hour bars and sex clubs. That passed behind too, and the line descended to ground-level — or, more likely, the ground rose to meet the line.

By the time a mechanical-sounding voice announced the terminus, the city was petering away to shabby tenements intermingled with warehouses. A distant roaring indicated that she was close to the airport through which EG dispatched its products, but that was out of sight behind a hill. There was a thick industrial stench in the air.

Uncertainly, she got out, last of the passengers to do so. There had only been three others in the car, a tired-eyed black woman and two black kids about twelve. Litter crunched under her sandals as she stepped on to the platform. Before her extended a street of grey buildings. Signs here and there identified small manufacturing companies making sanitary tampons, plastic cups, door-furniture. At the end of the street was a scrapyard where a tall crane was picking up metal on a magnet. The only person visible was pushing a hand-truck laden with garbage-cans, a sour-faced black.

She hesitated, glancing around. Nearby was a sales kiosk offering candies, cigarettes and porn. Its display window was of the old-fashioned intermittent-mirror type, and she caught sight of herself in it as it went into the reflecting phase. She stared with annoyance at her image. Her hair was exquisite, honey-gold; her face was oval, though not so perfect as to be dull. But there was an ill-tempered twist to her mouth, which she detested, yet which she could not help. She felt so furious with the world today.

Of course, she had come straight out of the apartment in what she happened to be wearing: playtop, shorts, sandals, and literally nothing else. It had been sheer luck that she'd had a pocketful of change. It would have been unbearable to go back for her wrist-purse.

Then the window cleared, and she realised she was being stared at by the owner of the kiosk, a fat middle-aged black. A tooth was missing in the centre of his grin. She spun on her heel at random and started down the street. She was just a little afraid. Yet the sensation was somehow stimulating. She felt she needed to do something terrible. Something that would shock the living shit out of her parents. Anything.

The concept took root in her mind, without words. It had the appeal of the suicide's note: 'You'll be sorry for what you made me do!'

And they had made her do it, hadn't they? Grandmother with her wood-rasp voice and her endless condemnation of young people today — well, she'd endured that all her life. But add in the nuisance of this newly-arrived Canadian, Holtzer, and the information that her abominable brother Peter was going to be crowded into her bedroom — they got on each other's nerves, and he was a reeky waster, and he'd left it until this morning to admit that he'd overspent his allowance and couldn't afford a hotel while Holtzer was here. . . Not that it was Holtzer's fault, of course; he seemed rather nice, with his square face, curly brown hair, and ready smile. But — damnation! If there was only one guest-room, and Grandmother was in it, and Dad *insisted* on accommodating this Canuck, why couldn't he move in with Mom? Lots of married people had gone back to sharing a room.

When she suggested it, her mother had given her a long steady stare. 'I shouldn't mention that to your father if I were you,' she'd said.

'Well, aren't you married?' had been Lora's caustic retort. And that began the row which drove her out.

She realised suddenly that while she was brooding a trio of young blacks had appeared at the end of the street, near the scrapyard gate, and they'd spotted her. For an instant she was minded to rush back on the platform; the

36

car was warming up for its return trip. Then she realised this was just the kind of thing she was after. She'd never had a black boy, let alone three of them at once.

Pausing after getting out of the hovercar, Magda Hansen looked down at the narrow concrete landing outside her apartment. There was a woman there — smartly dressed in dark blue, age indeterminate, heavily made-up, obviously wealthy and more likely to live in Lakonia than Cowville — who was wavering back and forth before the door. She poised her hand to press the bell, drew back, looked at the card saying CONSULTATIONS, made to turn away, and went through the whole cycle again.

Magda hoped fervently she would give up. But she didn't.

'Are you — are *you* Magda Hansen?' the woman said hesitantly, seeing her come down the stairs from the hoverhalt.

'Yes.' Magda shook back her coarse black hair and felt in her pocket for her key, the twin of Danty's. 'Why?'

'Well — uh — I'm Fenella Clarke. Avice Donnelly said I should come to you. She says you're absolutely wonderful.'

'Kind of her,' Magda sighed. 'So what do you want?'

'Help,' was the pathetic answer. 'And I don't know what kind.' She began to twist a platinum wedding-band around and around on her finger. 'It's — it's the way it was with Avice, more or less.'

It would be. But Magda kept her face straight.

'So I thought — uh — I ought to talk to you, too.'

'Very well. Shall we say Monday at three?'

Mrs Clarke's face fell. She said, 'I was hoping. . .'

'No, I'm sorry,' Magda cut in. 'You must know from Avice that I can't work a one-day miracle, and I have someone waiting inside right now.'

'But my husband. . .!' Fluttering her hands. 'You see, he's gone to the West Coast, but he comes back Monday.'

37

'He wouldn't approve?'

A helpless head-shake. Yes, that figured. If he was typical, he'd say at once, 'You're not to waste my money on a quack.'

'Perhaps you'd rather leave it until the next time he's away,' Magda suggested. 'Otherwise Monday really is the earliest I can offer.'

'Very well,' Mrs Clarke sighed, and turned away.

Danty was lying on one of the couches, eyes closed. Thinking him asleep, she entered quietly, but he heard her and called a greeting. She blew him a kiss and headed for the shower-stall. As she began to hang her clothes on a chair, she said, "How was it, Danty? Was it right?'

'Too right,' he answered, frowning. 'A man came out of the sea. And there was another man waiting to take him away in a car.'

'Wasn't that what you expected?'

'Yes!' Danty sat upright with a jerk. 'Yes, exactly! Magda, it's getting so accurate, I'm worried!'

'You'd be a lot more worried if you'd gone to that much trouble for something which didn't work out,' Magda said, and stepped into the shower. For the next couple of minutes the noise of water was too loud for conversation; besides, another hovercar pulled up and the building trembled.

Then she emerged, wrapped a towel around her, and sat down facing him. She said, 'I guess you've had enough time to make sense of what you saw?'

'Not really,' Danty muttered. 'What do you think?'

'An East Bloc agent being landed?'

'In a reserved area? Under the nose of radar and nuclear missiles? Jesus, *why?* For all their talk of security, the borders aren't tight — why not bring an agent in through Alaska, or Canada? The Cubans send theirs in through Mexico, don't they? Hell, the guy came out of the biggest submarine I ever saw, and if I —'

He stopped dead in mid-sentence. Magda tensed.

'Go on!' she encouraged.

He gave her a blank, helpless stare. 'I. . . Oh, I think sometimes I shall go insane! Do you know what I did? When I got through the fence, I — I *felt out* the equipment. I found the central switch-house, this little round thing made of that artificial ruby they use over in Lakonia, and I sneaked in and turned everything off. It's sort of complicated, but when you do it in a certain order. . . Well, never mind; I can't explain the details.

'But when I came away I *left* the site turned off!'

'Then they'll find out!' Magda exclaimed. 'They service those sites all the time — you see the helicopters taking off from the airport.'

'Yes, of course,' Danty said, staring miserably down at his hands. 'And I can feel that they'll find out soon. I had a reason for doing what I did, I'm sure of that. But I'll be radiated if I can remember what it was!'

'You're shaking, baby.' Magda said. 'Here! Let me wind you down.' She rose and began to strip off her towel.

'Uh-uh,' Danty sighed. 'It goes on.'

'What comes next?'

'I'm not sure. I only feel I have to be somewhere — out by the scrapyards on the west end of town. I'll know the spot when I get there.' He checked his watch. 'In fact it's about time I got started.'

'Have some pot, at least — or a trank, if you're really in a hurry.'

'No, I daren't risk it. I have to be as keyed up as I can.'

She stared at him for a long moment. Before she could say anything else, however, he had read her mind.

'You think I'm going to burn myself out, don't you?'

She gave a nod. A very slight nod, as though limiting the gesture could soften the truth behind it.

'Yes. Yes, I think so too,' Danty muttered. 'But not doing what I feel I have to do — that would be worse.' A faint smile followed the words. 'But thank you anyhow.

39

If there wasn't someone I could talk to, someone who cares about me, I'd have gone insane long ago.'

He rose, stretching. 'Although it's arguable, I guess,' he added, 'that I already am crazy. Poor Magda.'

'What?'

'Poor Magda, I said. Landed with one case for which you can't see any hopeful outcome.'

She pondered that, then shook her head. 'No, that's not true. You may burn yourself out, that's a fact. But it would be a very special kind of burning. Goodbye, Danty.'

7

'What ch'waiting fo'?' Potatohead muttered, staring at the addle cock blond with the bare chowbag. He nudged Josh Tatum.

'Poke me one more,' Josh said, 'I cut out yo' Idaho eyes. She walking this way? She climbing walls? Shee-*it*.'

Josh wasn't a reb and if you'd called him one he'd have carved you for it. They were tight on guns in Cowville but knives, everybody had knives. He was slick from neck to heel in plastic blacker than his skin, and shinier, and his scalp fuzzed an eighty-eight force-grown natural. Same with other, Shark Bance. Potatohead was shaved and ashamed. But something wrong with the follicles.

'Lakonia,' Shark said under his breath.

'Where the shit else? *I* know her.'

'What?'

'Name? *Name?* Piss her name. Peg it, *peg* it! Chow bare, zip-crotch shorts — eyes, use yo' *eyes!*'

'Pegged,' Potatohead said. 'Po' li'l rich, due fo' kindah-a surprise.' He grabbed Shark's hand and kissed it.

'Kill it! Wannah-a see that? She grunt pig! Spread an' bar-a walk. Makun quick!'

'Inta scrapyard?' Shark inquired.

'Scrapyard, yea.'

In spite of her resolution Lora felt nervous as she approached the young blacks. There was something so statue-like about them: all three tall, all three dead-faced, all three in that strange tight muscle-hugging plastic. . . She liked to feel a boy's skin before she let him unzip the crotch of her shorts, which was why she preferred the beach or in winter the dansoteks where it was always too hot for heavy clothing.

But this was the thing she had set her mind to, so she kept on going.

The nearest of them, with the shaven head, stepped into her path. She smiled sunnily at him and said, 'Hi!'

He looked at her with eyes as dull as pebbles. Then he reached out and touched, not her bare arm, but the fabric of her playtop. Meantime the one beside him, marginally the biggest, examined her critically from top to toe.

'In there,' he said after a couple of heartbeats, and jerked his head towards the scrapyard.

She was taken aback. This wasn't what she'd expected. There should be — well, a bit of chat. Banter. Joking. *Some* sort of preliminaries!

But they had fallen in around her like military police escorting a deserter, and were forcing her towards the scrapyard gate. There was a gatekeeper's hut. There was no one in it.

Huge clanging noises, and a sulphur stink. Horrified, she found herself shut in by walls of ruined cars, rusty bath-tubs, mounds of cans crushed into polychrome lumps, while underfoot she walked on painful glass.

'I —' she began to say, and they rounded a corner among the piles of metal and were out of sight of anyone.

'Value her,' the tallest black said, and the bald one confronted her and took her wrist. He inspected her watch.

'Saw, Josh?' the third said. 'No purse!'

'Saw,' the tallest said. 'Zip up, Shark. Well, Potato-head?'

'Piss and shit! Japanese! Worth around eight-fifty!'

'Foreign, um? Ah-hunh! Anna clothes?'

'Three-fo' hunnad inna sto'. Top getcha mayba fifty. Shorts widda zip crotch, dustin'-rag.'

'Takun fo' pock't. I see coin. Strippun, addle.'

As though by magic a long knife appeared in Josh's hand

42

and touched Lora's bosom with a cold caress.

'But — but what. . .?' Words choked her. It wasn't that she didn't understand the order (addle: adolescent; they said that in Lakonia, too). She didn't understand the situation.

Slowly, and with immaculate diction, Josh said, 'Strip, cock. We don't want to get blood on those clothes.'

She stared at him for a terrible empty moment, thinking: *cock means Caucasian, and that's only used by. . .*

It dawned on her at long last what they meant to do. Rob her, and kill her, and hide her body among the scrap.

'Knahf, blabboh. Droppun knahf.'

A voice from nowhere. Josh whirled around, eyes vastly wide. He, they, Lora spotted the speaker almost in the same moment: high on top of the pile of scrap overlooking them, a dark face peering down, cheek cuddled close to the significant tube of a rifle.

'Knahf!' the voice repeated. 'O' takun ow-yo' han' wiffa slug, blabboh!'

There was an eternity of frozen silence. All Lora could think of was that only one black man could call another blabboh — 'black boy' — and survive.

Then Josh, mouth curled as though he had bitten a lemon, opened his fingers and let the knife fall.

'Addle cock!' the stranger said sharply. 'Back slo' — tutri pesses — so'sa fahn. Narrunda co'nah — fahn again!'

As in a dream, Lora reacted to the half-understood order, backing around the corner of the stack of scrap.

'Okay,' the gunman said, and then added, more loudly and with a forced blabboh intonation: 'Ah seeah! Slongzah seeah Ah c'nitchah! Mango blabboh, mango!'

A gesture with his rifle. And they went.

Half a minute later, while Lora was sobbing into her hands, a tug on her arm. 'Move it!'

Gone was the blabboh accent, but the same voice. She

opened her eyes to see her rescuer — lean, young, dark, not as black as her captors but black nonetheless — tossing his rifle aside.

'But they might come after us!' she cried.

'Sure. I said move it, didn't I?' Catching her by the arm and literally dragging her along.

'But the gun — !'

'Not worth a fart. Picked out of a stack of them over there. Military surplus. Empty! Will you *move?*'

He led her stumbling through the awful man-made desert of the scrapyard, to a gap in the perimeter fence, down a narrow alley. . . By that time she was gasping for breath, and barely registered where he was taking her. Then around a corner, and after a quick survey of the street in both directions — just such a street as she'd emerged on to from the hoverhalt — at a quieter pace for another few hundred yards, his arm around her waist now, his hand companionable on her bare skin.

'It's over now,' he said, close to her ear. 'But you got a scare, that's for sure. You over the legal?'

'Uh. . .' For a moment she didn't understand, although the coarse blabboh accent had faded from his speech and he was speaking precisely as might any of her friends. Then she saw a bar-sign ahead. Yes, a drink. A stiff shot of — anything. She said so. Her voice not only sounded but felt like someone else's.

In the bar, a couple of black men at the counter gave them a dull once-over, then reverted to their liquor. He brought her brandy, and beer for himself. Sitting down opposite her across a table with a chipped plastic top, he said, 'Drink it. Then breathe as deeply as you can, ten times. I'll wait.'

It worked, somehow. Maybe it was the confidence in his tone. Her heart, which had been slamming to let out through her ribs, slowed to a more normal rate, and she was able to look at her new friend properly. Some tune she didn't recognise battered her ears; she had only just realised music was playing. As though the episode in the scrapyard had not happened she found herself thinking: *Yes, I hoped to meet a black boy like this, tough, lean, crooked smile, graceful-moving. . .*

And — ?

There was a stern reproach in his eyes. He said, 'When you come here, learn to pick your kicks.'

'I. . . She swallowed hard. 'I didn't think they. . .'

'Yea, yea,' he cut in. 'But — *shit!* None of them three looked twice at a girl in their lives, 'cept maybe to peel her down.'

She looked miserably at her empty glass and nodded.

He gave his crooked smile again and patted her hand. 'So okay, no harm done. Just don't make the same mistake twice. By the way, my name's Danty.'

'Mine's Lora,' she said distractedly. 'Lora Turpin. Uh —'

But Danty had tensed. He leaned forward. 'Not Turpin of Energetics General?'

'Why. . . Why, yes. Do you — ?'

'Know him? Shit, no. Heard of him though.' And in the manner of an afterthought: 'Friends of mine work at EG.'

Which she had imagined to be all of Cowville, the building to incorporate the city. She touched her bosom where the point of Josh's knife had rested, and a shiver racked her.

'You not? No? What *do* you do?'

'My best to be myself,' Danty murmured, and sipped beer.

Recognition signals. Landmarks. Like knowing (because a TV programme had said so with authority) that only queer blacks close to farming stock called white teenage girls 'addle cocks'. She said explosively, 'Are you a *reb?*'

'I guess I wouldn't cross the road to contradict you.'

She stared at him, and went on staring. Now and then, the other side of New Lake, the son or daughter of some wealthy family put on the reb-style pose, and that was

where it stopped — just a pose. According to the social
history she had been drilled through in school, every
generation for centuries had had its rebs, clear back to the
wandering students of the Middle Ages. But something
kept on going, fed from a source she couldn't understand.
Once, in an essay, she'd spoken of a humanistic counterpart of divine discontent — the phrase borrowed from a
book not on the curriculum — and she'd been marked
down two grades for saying it.

'You?' he was asking. 'You in college?'

'Uh. . .' Remembering with an effort. 'I go to college
in the fall. Just finished school.'

And what would it be like, there at Bennington?

An odd feeling, as though she were two people at once.
At home she had been allowed to drink since she was
fourteen, so it couldn't be the brandy which had hit her.
It must be shock. She half wanted to cry, and half wanted
to laugh hysterically.

'And what brought you here?' Danty said.

So she told him: words flooding out, tumbling over
each other, confusing the argument she wanted to frame,
until she was certain he must think her mentally deranged.
Yet he sat there, and nodded now and then, and heard her
out.

He said eventually, 'You like to night-ride, I guess.'

'Oh, yes!' (Black sky, black road, the universe conden-
sed to a pattern of lights, the ever-present expectation —
hope? — of 'instant death': *just add blood.)*

'Yes.' Nodding. 'It's the idea of going somewhere. To
look for something you might not recognise if you found
it. Only the places you most want to go, they won't let
you.'

She was about to say that was *exactly* what she felt,
when she realised with a pang of shame that she'd clean
forgotten to tell him something very important.

'Danty! Oh, Jesus! I didn't thank you!'

'Not to worry.'

46

'But —!' Now she was shaking all over again, from a different cause. 'But you must think I'm awful! And it was fantastic what you did, really incredible! Danty, you're kind of a terrific person.'

'I'm myself,' he said, and drained his glass.

'But — oh, *shit!*' Well, it was the only way she knew to say thanks properly, so with her hand hovering over her crotch-zip: 'Do you have somewhere we could. . .? You know!'

'Place but not time. Thanks all the same. Shall I show you to a hoverhalt?' Making to rise.

No, it can't stop here! I mean: SAVED MY LIFE!
'No, wait!' Mind racing. And then inspiration. *Oh, yes! Just the right hit to blow the minds, turn up with a black reb!* 'Hey, look! We have this big party for tomorrow night, this real stand-up-and-grin-if-it-chokes-you affair! Can I send you an invitation? I mean — oh, Danty, I do want to see you again!'

He nodded and settled back in his seat, pulling a pen from his pocket.

'Why not? Here's my address, inasmuch as I have one.'

8

Feeling almost ashamed of herself because she hadn't been this excited about a party for years, Lora took special care before her mirror, selecting her best makeup and perfume, then deliberately putting on a dress her father hated, a harlequin rig of lozenge-shaped bits of cloth tacked together only at the corners which showed as much of her as it concealed.

No doubt that meant that some of Dad's friends would try to feel her up, and she didn't intend to put out for reeky old turds like them, but if Danty *did* show. . .

'Here's my address, inasmuch as I have one.' *Wow.*

The house-phone rang. It was her mother.

'Lora honey, would you fix me a drink?'

She stamped her small foot. 'Can't you send Estelle?'

'Well, she's fixing my hair right now.'

'Oh! Oh, all right.' In a sullen tone. But she was all through dressing, and Peter might show up any minute, so getting out of the room was not a bad idea --

And here he came, panicking, starting to throw his outdoor clothes all over everywhere as usual. She headed promptly for the door.

'Don't let me drive you out, sister mine!' he exclaimed. 'You saw me take my pants off before, didn't you?'

'Going to fix Mom a drink,' Lora said, sweeping by.

'Me too!' Peter cried. 'I'm in a rush.'

'That's your fault,' Lora snapped, and strode away.

The nearest liquor cabinet was in her father's room. The The room was empty. She mixed a gin atomic for her mother and a weak Bloody Mary for herself, and went next door where Mrs Turpin sat naked at her mirror while her French-Canadian maid set out accessories to go with her radion gown.

'Thanks, honey,' she said in a strangled tone due to the need to let her lip-shade dry without wrinkling. 'Put a straw in it for me, Estelle.'

'Mind if I drink mine here?' Lora said. 'If I go back in my room Peter will grab it. And by the way!'

'Yes?'

'You couldn't arrange to have his drinks watered to-. night, could you? He's bad enough sober. When he's drunk — Christ!'

'Oh, he won't try and rape you, if that's what you mean,' her mother said calmly.

'Mom! That's beyond joking!' Lora gasped.

'Unfortunately it is. But the fact stands: you're a girl. And, come to think of it, you seem to want everyone to be absolutely certain. Are you seriously going to wear that bunch of rags, if you can call it wearing?'

'Why not?' With a gulp of her drink.

'Well, your father — but I guess that's why you put it on. More important, I asked Reverend Powell to be here sharp on time, and I don't want him to see you dressed like a whore.'

'Don't make me laugh! He made a pass at me last time he was here, the slimy slug.'

'Well, he doesn't pretend to be above temptation — that's one reason people like him. But don't let me hear you call him a slug again, understood? Or I'll forget you're eighteen and whop you blue. I won't have you bad-mouthing a minister. And one more thing! Don't spend the evening like you usually do, moping around some plastic-headed boy. Mix! Talk to people — '

'I'll spend the whole radiated night with anyone I choose,' Lora said, and slammed the door.

After that, she didn't really want to join the line-up at

49

the entrance to the party hall. That was a room about sixty feet by eighty, shared between their apartment and the next; there was one on each floor of the tower, and doors off it were unlocked according to which family were the hosts.

But she was afraid of missing Danty if she didn't.

So she waited until her father was busy greeting an early guest, then darted into a spot beside Holtzer, thinking that even if Dad did want to slang her for wearing this dress he'd hardly do so in a stranger's hearing. She was right, and escaped with a mere scowl.

Holtzer, on the other hand, looked her over thoughtfully and at leisure, and said at last, 'You look lovely, Lora.'

'Well, thank you,' she murmured, because he'd said it in a tone that made her believe it. She relaxed — but only for a heartbeat or two, because here suddenly came Peter in a hideous party-suit of yellow lace and stinking to the sky. He rushed to his mother, lying about how he hadn't been able to get ready sooner because his reeky sister was underfoot, but Mrs Turpin was used to that and froze him fast.

'It's your preening and primping that takes the time!' she snapped. 'Get yourself a drink and shut up!'

Instantly furious, Peter was about to scream back at her, but that was the moment when Reverend Powell arrived: a fine-looking man with a commanding presence which had made him the highest-paid TV evangelist in history. And, of course, Peter pounced on him.

Well, that's one way of avoiding the two people I least want on my back. . . Lora sighed, and found Holtzer looking at her again. This time he winked, and she grinned back. Good to know there was one other person here who wasn't dazzled by this parade of notables, these generals, admirals, senators, TV stars and other slugs. Plus, naturally, the whole of the EG Board.

But she had to be polite, for the time being.

The crush increased tremendously within minutes. Even in Lakonia people had got out of the habit of arriving at parties late and staying late. Going home after midnight wasn't as risky here as in New York, Washington or LA — where most parties nowadays were held in the afternoon — but the pattern was contagious.

Abruptly the racket of conversation dwindled to a buzz, and Sheklov, surprised, glanced towards the door. Two men with blue jowls and stern expressions were coming in. They ignored the host and hostess, but walked silently around the assembly, sharp eyes piercing and probing.

'Well!' someone he didn't know said beside Sheklov. 'So Prexy *is* coming!'

'How do you — ?' Sheklov began, and then put two and two together. 'Oh. Secret Service?' A chill touched his nape.

'Yes,' the stranger said importantly. 'Those are Crashaw and Levitt. They're alleged to have by heart the entire CIA and FBI files on subversives. See how tense the Turpin girl is? Worried in case they tell Prexy not to come in!'

Lora caught that and glanced over her shoulder with a scowl. *Fool!* she thought. There was someone she was far more concerned about than Prexy — and here he was!

She had had vague visions of him arriving with a dozen reb friends, leaping with a whoop and a holler into the middle of this stuffy crowd and blowing every mind for miles. But, instead, he was quietly taking in the scene from the threshold, neatly if not expensively dressed in wine-red, not seeming at all out of place except that his complexion was the darkest in view.

He saved my life! she thought again, savouring the solidity of the concept, and ran to kiss him. Several people noticed. They were meant to.

Sheklov was staying close to Turpin. That suited his

51

rôle as a stranger who knew almost no one, but also it was safer, because although his briefing had been thorough he was not yet primed with current gossip.

He was impressed. Turpin's assimilation was unbelievably complete. People were present who made the headlines simply by catching a head-cold. And even those secret service agents had looked Turpin in the face, never suspecting that he had been born in the *other* Georgia – that he had grown up answering to the name of Yashvili — that it had taken four years' planning and three deaths to turn him into Lewis Raymond Turpin, known inevitably as 'Dick' . . .

Sheklov suddenly recalled something which Bratcheslavsky had repeated many times during his briefing: 'Don't let his assimilation put you off. Bear in mind it saved the world!'

True enough. Every circuit in 'the world's most perfect defensive system' had been known to Turpin for years. He didn't sabotage the installations, or even delay them — that wasn't his job. All he did was pass the news on.

Yes, by doing that he'd saved the world. But Sheklov thought of an alien ship sparkling near Pluto, and wondered with a shiver: *For how long?*

An outburst of clapping, and there he was, clasping his hands above his head like a boxer. A photographer accompanying him snapped a shot for tomorrow's papers. He was a large man, broad-faced, broad-shouldered, broad-grinning. As Turpin approached, beaming, he dropped his hands and changed his grin for his look of sincere pleasure, and the photographer snapped again.

Sheklov hung back, watching intently. A dozen people had actually entered the hall, but all bar Prexy had expertly effaced themselves. That wasn't hard; guests were pressing forward, determined to shake the famous hand or at least to be told hello. Sheklov had heard about this phenomenon, but until now had barely believed it. Yes, they did worship this figurehead, this waxwork, this mindless creation of a skilled team of Navy publicists!

Don't they know what's been done to them? Or is it that they don't care?

Now Turpin was signalling him, and he had to move forward, other guests reluctantly permitting him passage.

'Prexy! I'd like you to meet a friend of mine from Canada, Don Holtzer here.'

Prexy was instantly Prexy-to-the-nth. 'Dick, any friend of yours is a friend of mine, and any friend of mine is a friend of the USA. Mr Holtzer. Or rather, Don.'

He offered his hand, beaming. Sheklov took it. The photographer snapped, snapped again, and glanced up. 'Say, Mr Turpin. That young lady's your daughter? Like to have her in a shot or two as well, a spot of glam.'

The scene seemed to freeze. At length Turpin said, 'Lora?'

She came forward unwillingly, holding her boy-friend tight by the hand. "Only if he's in the shot too," she said.

'And why not?' A boom from Prexy. 'Here, young lady! A kind of parable for us all, isn't it? I've never been able to hold against them the resentment some of our darker fellow-citizens feel — justifiably, if you look at the historical record. I hope and pray for the day when we shall resolve our disagreements peacefully. And for you and your compatriots, Don, the same thing holds. One's aware there have been differences, one's aware that relations between our countries are not as happy as they have been right now, but bonds of honest trade still forge links between our lands, and where business binds friendship follows, sooner or later — '

Meantime he was putting his arm around Lora and hopefully trying to insert his fingers through the slots of her dress, but she obviously was not one of the many who felt it a privilege to be touched by Prexy. The fact that she wriggled away, however, did not disconcert him in the slightest. Snap. He altered his pose with practised skill. Snap again. Sheklov stood numb, wearing a feeble grin. He was terribly aware of the eyes of Crashaw and Levitt fixed on him, saying without words: 'We'll know you next time we see you.'

Snap once more, and finished. As though a spell had been lifted, people started moving about and talking as loudly as before, while Turpin found Prexy a drink and ushered him towards the densest part of the crowd, his favourite spot. Watching him go, Sheklov heard again that slick alliterative catch-phrase — 'where business binds friendship follows' — and felt briefly haunted by the ghosts of a million Asian peasants.

He realised abruptly that he was being stared at. By the young man Lora had insisted on pulling into the photograph with her, the lean black, the only black here. Blacks didn't make it to Lakonia, he'd been told.

The instant he met that dark gaze, it flicked away. But it left a dismayingly deep dent, for no apparent reason, in his hitherto impermeable composure.

9

After that music began, and Sheklov had to circulate.
Almost at once he had an alarming encounter with a TV
producer named Ambow, who was eager for praise of
some historical-drama series he had made. Sheklov, not
having seen the show, had no opinion at first, but by the
time Ambow found a more promising victim he had a
very firm opinion indeed. The series was decadent bourgeois non-representational escapism of the worst conceivable kind. A man like Ambow couldn't possibly
create anything better.

Indeed, this whole function had a curious quasi-
historical air. The tunes being played, for example, dated
back fifteen, even twenty-five years, and in the identical
style of their originals. The clothes, too, struck him as
subtly behind the times — what you might have seen at a
Kremlin reception a decade ago. Growing more and more
depressed, he drifted from one group to another, and
heard lectures on the Spics ('A billion bucks we spent on
aid, and the Cubans put 'em in their pocket!'), on the
Gooks ('All those American boys who died trying to save
them from the Reds!'), and the Black Africans ('Can't
trust anyone over there except the Boers, and I don't
think we do enough for them!') . . .

I didn't believe it, he thought. *But it's true!*

He wondered whether someone like Ambow, working
with material from the past, recognised the analogies you
could draw, one-for-one, with other places and other
times. And concluded that if anyone did, he must prefer
to ignore them. It made him desperately sad.

Eventually, passing the half-open door which led into the living-room of the Turpins' apartment, he heard a familiar sound.

'Well, well,' he murmured under his breath. 'Prokofiev!'

He debated for a moment whether it was in character for Holtzer to like 'The Love of Three Oranges', and decided that that was irrelevant. Shrugging, he pushed open the door. Beyond, the lights were down to a dim glow, but he had been in here earlier today and thought he knew the layout well enough not to turn them up. He headed for a chair facing the player. It was not until he almost fell over an outstretched leg that he realised the room's long lounge, end-on to the door, was occupied by Lora and her dark-skinned friend. She was crawling all over him, but although his hands were inside her dress, fondling her back, he didn't seem to be acting very passionately.

'Sorry,' he murmured, and made to withdraw.

And backed straight into a tall, good-looking man with a shock of sleek grey hair, who in the same moment snapped the lights to full.

'Oh, Lora!' he exclaimed. 'Do you know what's become of your brother?'

'Shit, piss and *damnation*,' Lora said in a weary tone, and rolled off Danty, flinging her legs angrily to the floor. 'No, I don't! I'm not my brother's keeper, thank God!'

The handsome man reddened, and Sheklov placed him; he'd been pointed out as a minister of religion. Powers? No, Powell, that was it: Maurice Powell.

'Hey, Don,' Lora added, seeing that Sheklov was on the point of leaving the room. 'Don't run off!'

Sheklov halted on the threshold. There was a pause. Eventually Powell gave an insincere grin and went out.

'Oh, that *slug*!' Lora said, falling back on the couch. Danty had twisted around into a sitting position and reached for a glass on a nearby table. 'Put the lights

56

down again, Don, and have a chair.'

'I don't want to interrupt — ' Sheklov began.

'Zip it!' she interrupted with a harsh laugh. 'That's
one of *his* lines. Know what he did to me, last party he
came to here? Walked right into my bedroom where I
was making out with somebody, sat down and started
playing with himself while he watched. Christ, he makes
my *skin* crawl!'

She seized and lit a cigarette from the table.

'Still, as long as he knows you're in here, he won't
come back. Or with luck he'll find Peter. Made for each
other, those two . . . Shit, I forgot. Danty, this is Don
Holtzer.'

'We almost met,' Danty said with a crooked grin. 'In
the pic with Prexy.'

'Yes, of course,' Lora muttered. 'Jesus, Danty, how
does that hit you?'

'Like dry ice.' Danty set his glass aside again. 'You're
from Canada, aren't you, Don?'

On edge for some indefinable reason — maybe because
of the searching quality of the stare Danty had given him
before — Sheklov nodded. 'Yes, I'm in timber up there.
Manitoba.'

That much was absolutely safe to say. There were
scores of Canadian firms ready to give Russian agents
cover, and he had a genuine deal to conclude.

'I'd like to go north some time,' Lora said. She
realised that her left nipple was showing through one of
the gaps in her dress, and tugged a lozenge of cloth back
into place. 'There's something rather cultural about
Canada, I think.'

Sheklov blinked, experiencing the sensation of being
displaced backward in time more acutely than ever. How
long since *kulturny* ceased to be a fad-word Back There?
Ten years? Twenty?

'What makes you say that?' he inquired, honestly
curious.

'Well — uh — its links with European tradition. Speaking French there, for one thing.' Lora's answer had a seizing-at-straws sound. 'Mother's maid Estelle is from Montreal, and she speaks French. I think it's a romantic language.'

Obviously, having recovered from her annoyance at failing to get all the way with Danty, she was sliding into a regular rôle. Now she added in a wistful tone, 'I've often dreamed of standing on the Champs Elysées and watching the sun go down behind the Arc de Triomphe.''

'You'd have a long wait,' Danty said.

She glared at him. 'Shit, you know what I *mean*!'

But Sheklov's nape had suddenly begun to prickle. Danty had uttered that statement with authority. And it was quite correct; if you were standing in the Champs Elysées, the sun couldn't set behind the Arc de Triomphe. He said, before Lora could go on, 'You've been there, have you?'

'How would I get a passport?' Danty grunted, and turned to his drink again.

Yet there had been assurance in his tone . . .

Still, Lora was talking again. 'Have you travelled much, Don? It's easier for Canadians, isn't it?'

'Well, I guess so,' Sheklov said, mentally reviewing Holtzer's life-story. 'But me, I haven't been around too much. We're one of the few countries left with a frontier, you know. Pushing north instead of west. That gives us a lot of elbow-room. So we —'

The door, which Powell had closed on leaving, slammed wide, and there in the opening was Peter. Obviously he had been drinking heavily; he was flushed and unsteady on his feet.

'Well, well!' he exclaimed. 'That's so sweet! My sister and her johnnyreb snuggled up.'

'Zip your mouth, you reeky turd,' Lora said, and twisted on the couch so her back was towards her brother.

'Hey!' Sheklov exclaimed, half-rising. A look of instant fury had appeared on Peter's face, and he seemed about to launch himself bodily at Lora.

'Oh, fade away!' she told him over her shoulder.

'Peter?' a richly resonant voice said from outside. Yes, it was Powell back again. 'Ah, there you are!' He touched the boy companionably on the arm, and left his hand there as Peter stepped back against him.

'I'm going to make you pay for that!' he snarled at Lora.

'Peter!' Powell reproved. 'That's no way to talk to —'

'So how would you like to be called a reeky turd?'

'Oh, sticks and stones, you know, sticks and stones!' Having located Peter again, Powell seemed to have had his good humour restored too. He eased the boy into a chair and sat on its arm, his hand still where he had first put it. 'I must say the party's going splendidly, isn't it? Are you enjoying yourself, Lora?'

'In the company of my johnnyreb, yes, thank you!'

'My dear girl!' Powell said, shocked. 'That's not a term to bandy around lightly, you know. To call someone a reb is to accuse him of being a wastrel, whose actions strike at the very foundations of our cherished heritage.'

And Danty glanced up and nodded; '*Mm-hm!*'

That threw Powell completely. He almost gaped for a moment, and then added, making a fast comeback, 'Though we must not condemn too harshly. It's not for us to sit in judgment, after all.'

'Except on ourselves,' Danty murmured, and packed a dozen personal implications into the comment. Powell got them all. He tugged at his clerical collar as though it were suddenly too tight.

'Very true. I must remember that phrase. "Sermons in stones. . . " And we're told that stony ground will be the lot of some of our seed. Tell me, young man, are you lapsed from the brotherhood of your church?'

'I guess so,' Danty said indifferently.

'Shame! But we mustn't lose hope for you, must we? "There is more joy in heaven — " And so on.'

Maliciously Danty said, 'And so on — what?'

' "Over one sinner that repenteth", ' Powell answered automatically. Then he realised he was being needled. He rose.

'Pardon me,' he said with a half-bow. 'I'm a long-suffering man, but I can't endure mockery of my Cloth. Come, Peter. I think I begin to understand your antipathy to your sister.'

The instant the door closed, Lora threw herself at Danty. 'Oh, you're wonderful!' she cried, and thrust her tongue into his ear. 'I'll go find some more drinks — I want to wash away the taste of that slug. Won't be long.'

And, rising, she added to Sheklov, 'What's yours, Don? Whisky? Right!'

Left alone with Danty, Sheklov thought himself by main force back into the conservatively disapproving rôle which fitted his pose as a successful Canadian salesman, and said, 'You told the minister you're a reb. I hope you were only — uh — needling him?'

Danty gave a shrug. 'Well, I didn't invent the term, but I find it easy to put on.'

Sheklov's mind raced. How to strike a balance between ostensible conformity and real interest? Once again he recalled Bratcheslavsky, squatting on the floor in distant Alma-Ata; the old man had said 'Reb!' That's a word to bear in mind. There's something going on. From here one can't find out exactly what. Official smog surrounds the reality. Maybe it's just another term for what we used to call *stilyagi*, or jet-set. On the other hand, maybe not.'

He felt suddenly dizzy. Those dark eyes were boring into his again. Could the liquor — ? No, of course not. It was far weaker than the 140-proof Polish vodka he . . .

From a very great distance a voice that was recognisably Danty's reached him. It was saying, 'You want I should join the church Powell runs? Twenty million people watch his sermons every Sunday. That makes *him* a holy man?'

And then the appalling, incredible thing happened. He continued,' "Those who are full of desires for self-gratification, regarding paradise as their highest goal, and are engaged in many intricate scriptural rites just to secure pleasure and power as the result of their deeds for their future incarnations — " '

And Sheklov went on with it. He couldn't help it. *He couldn't help it.* Cold terror raged through him at every funeral-bell syllable that he uttered, but he heard his own voice, out of control, inexorably finishing the quotation.

' "Whose discrimination is stolen away by the love of power and pleasure and who are thus deeply attached therein, for such people it is impossible to obtain either firm conviction or God-consciousness." '

Sweat crawled on his palms. The last time he had heard that truth, it had been in another language, in Banaras, and Donald Holtzer had never been to India.

That was his cover blown to bits.

10

Later, he got extremely drunk. His cover as Holtzer was
proof against that — it had been tried to the limit during
training sessions — and anyway the same thing was
happening to a lot of other people, starting with Prexy,
who fell down at about eleven-thirty and had to be discreetly removed. Then there was a curious blurred inter-
lude involving two women who claimed the right to go to
bed with Turpin because their husbands were necking
with each other. He didn't follow the logic of that, but
it came to blows, and one of them departed with a
swollen eye which would call for her best cosmetic skills
tomorrow.

Yet everyone was shaking Turpin's hand, or kissing his
wife, or both, with enormous warmth, and saying, 'Mar-
vellous party, Dick! You must come to our place very
soon.'

*What's the standard of a 'good party'? The fact that
no one was taken to the hospital?*

Danty and Lora had disappeared early. Something
about a night-ride? He wasn't sure, but he hoped —

Do I? He struggled to think through the alcoholic haze,
and concluded that he hoped yes. If they were drunk
enough to crash into a bridge on the superway, that
would rescue him from his terror. In this country for a
matter of hours, and already betrayed by his own stupid-
ity! He felt as though he had exposed himself on the
street, knowing there was a policeman within shouting
distance.

Ultimately, a little before the last guests left at one

o'clock, he found his way to the room he'd been allotted — normally Peter's — and screamed at a group of three men and two women using the bed. They went away, spitting at him, and he collapsed.

And then he had to fight his hangover.

The maid Estelle came silently to him at nine with a remedy of some sort, a pill fizzing in a glass of water. Apparently it was the routine after-party treatment in the Turpin household. Five minutes later he felt a little better.

He sat up in bed, sipping the coffee which she had also brought, and used the remote-control to turn down the TV. She had switched it on, without asking him, as she went out. He'd already noticed that these extraordinary people didn't seem to feel that a room was habitable unless either bland music or a TV image were included in the décor.

He postponed consideration of his self-revelation to Danty, because on the one hand the subject was too complex to analyse while he was hung over, and on the other although he felt the sky had fallen on him he had not yet been hauled away to a cell.

Of course, by his standards this room could have done duty for one; it was larger by a bare metre in each direction than the bed. . . though there were closets built into the wall.

He shook his head incredulously. Two hundred thousand dollars! That was what his briefing said Turpin had had to pay for this — this rabbit-hutch! And his was only in the medium range. The most expensive apartments here had two extra rooms and a party-hall that didn't have to be shared, and set the buyer back twice as much. But you didn't aspire to that unless you were on the Energetics General Board or of staff rank in the armed forces. In this particular tower, Sheklov knew, the penthouse belonged to a four-star Air Force general.

How did a nation *get* into a mess like this?

So far he hadn't managed to explore this one city, let alone the surrounding country, but he had been thoroughly stuffed with data, and against the throbbing of his head he fought to organise what he recalled into some sort of relevance to his situation. Lots of glib catch-phrases came to mind, for example: 'Human beings are subject to forces so ingrained in their thinking as to render them incapable of detached evaluation of their own behaviour.'

Very helpful. In other words: 'All we learn from history' — or psychology, or anthropology, or ethnology — *'is that we learn nothing from history'* — or psychology, or. . .

Yes.

Still, these people had learned how to make a first-rate anti-hangover pill. He was already able to look directly at the brightly sunlit window of the room without narrowing his eyes. No doubt of it, Lakonia offered some lovely views — those towers like a solemn crazy forest, the sparkling lake, the redwoods in the distance which, force-grown or not, were splendid trees, rivalling anything he had seen in Siberia.

And their Chief Executive (nominal ruler) had been carried out, dead drunk, from the room adjacent . . .

Bewildered, he shook his head. It had to be an illusion! You couldn't possibly run a country this way.

Liar, his conscience said. *It's being done. So you can.*

At which point his more orthodox attitudes overcame him: *Yes, but look at the trouble it causes everyone else!*

He heaved an enormous sigh, told himself the hangover pill was perfect, superb, terrific, and finally managed to whip the crazy ringing nonsense inside his skull into some sort of pattern. It was a dismayingly random pattern — a mental counterpart of decadent non-representational

64

art — but it had some expressionist overtones he found comforting because they indicated that he was at least beginning to feel, instead of just perceiving, the functionality of the extraordinary society he was visiting.

To begin with, this is NOT the Eastern Roman Empire. The hell with how many parallels you can draw! (Who am I? Oh, that's not hard to define. I'm the discontented mercenary within the gates, who has taken sufficient pay in coin stamped with the Emperor's head — or rather, with the heads of Emperors, because they change their rulers like the weather — to lie indolent on the triclinium and open his mouth to the food offered by a domestic whore. Male or female.) POW!

A stab of pain lanced his forehead over his left eye; the hangover pill wasn't, obviously, a hundred per cent efficient. He gulped more coffee and wondered wistfully what would have become of America if it had socialised cannabis instead of alcohol.

Resuming: *In that case, the hungry Huns at the gates of the Empire are —*

'Oh, stop it!' he said aloud, and slapped his bare thigh. One didn't wear pyjamas or nightshorts here; according to his briefing, the mere possession of such garments was taken as proof of lack of confidence in one's ability to secure a partner for the night . . . of one sort or another. (He still didn't entirely believe the cover which, Turpin had assured him, excused his overnight absence from home in order to collect a spy from the sea. The story was that Turpin now and then liked to sleep with a man, and because of his professional standing preferred to travel a long way from Lakonia to look for one. And never talked about where he had spent the night, and never asked what his wife had done while he was away.)

Did that brown-skinned 'reb' Danty slip me a psyche-delic drug last night? I feel as though . . .

But a glance at his watch, not removed because he'd

been briefed concerning Americans' attitudes to time and knew he would be suspect if he was caught without a watch even while making love, confirmed that since he swallowed the first mouthful of his coffee only two minutes had gone by. The illusion that he had spent ages musing like this stemmed simply from the impression that he had been shouted at, non-stop, since he came ashore. He had met more people last night, for instance, in a shorter space of time, than ever before in his life, and digesting such a storm of information was like eating a nine-course banquet directly after fasting for a week. Mental eructations interrupted every argument he tried to think through to a conclusion.

One more try!

His coffee-cup was empty. He thought about pressing the buzzer by his bed, which would bring back Estelle to see what he wanted. That was among the reasons why an apartment in the Lakonia towers was so expensive; no other dwellings had been erected in the United States for over twenty years which incorporated a room for a servant and facilities for summoning her. Besides, there was almost literally nowhere else where anyone willing to be a servant would voluntarily seek employment. No native American would do so; Canadians were scarce; Mexicans were allowed in only on sufferance, by way of consolation for having their country policed by US soldiers, and so many Cuban saboteurs had sneaked in by posing as Puerto Rican valets and chambermaids that a total ban had been imposed.

(It was like being the focal point of a beam of light split up between the facets of a jewel, then reflected back towards a centre by a ring of distorting mirrors. He was aware, simultaneously, of the things he had been told in his briefings Back There, and of the things he had seen which matched his briefings, and also of the things which didn't — and these last were terrifying.)

Get your head straight! (And, superimposed, aware-

ness of the fact that the phrase was older than he was.)
Take it from the top!

So where is the top? Government level? Good enough.
Here I am: the cherry on the sundae of the Frozen War.

Was anyone still trying to break that twenty-year-old
international log-jam? Since they recalled and jailed the
American negotiators in Canberra, for collaborating with
the enemy, surely someone must have had another go?
Tonga? Was that where the conference last — ?

Oh, never mind. For all practical purposes, you had to
compute with the status-quo. In other words, these people knew that their country had been the first to put men
on the moon, and capped that achievement by doing it a
second time, and then discovered that there were two
billion other people who didn't give a damn about the
moon. Too late. Just in time to pull the troops back and
assign them to the streets of American cities. If they'd
waited a year longer, there wouldn't have been troops to
pull back. Whole army corps had been decimated by
desertion, exactly as happened to the Tsarist armies in
1917.

Then there was a slump, which rendered American
corporations unable to meet overseas commitments.
Then, because of the slump, there was a witch-hunt, and
the possession of an American passport became the (high-
priced) excuse to apply for political asylum elsewhere.
The end result was, simply, that no one wanted to know
the Americans any more, and the Americans stuck their
noses in the air and said, 'Stuff you, Jack, we're self-
sufficient.'

Like the Byzantine Empire after the loss of the rich
western provinces to the barbarians.

But only *like* that. Not the *same*! True, they talked in
similar terms, forever complaining about the foreigners
who bit the hand which fed them, and they treated their
fellow-creatures as objects — thus to lie with a woman
was a mere discharge of tension, not the gage of a genuine

liking. But there hadn't been an empire. The tentacles of what might have become one had been chopped off just in time — by the Vietnamese, the Cambodians, the Burmese, the Filipinos, all of them with help from Peking.

Nonetheless the *kalpa* was cycling. He could feel it. He had studied Marx; he had studied Toynbee and Sorokin; he had studied the *Rig-Veda*. It was his firm conviction that the resources of human beings were limited, and that implied that — even if there were no precise repetition — a man now, in a predicament analogous to that of a man ten thousand years ago, would react in an analogous manner. The Hindu notion that the universe repeated itself was a poetic truth, like the Toynbeean parable of the progress of civilisation. He, like everyone else, was carried on a wave in the middle of an ocean too vast to discern the shores of, and. . .

And it was making him sea-sick. He got off the bed with a grunt of anger and went to see whether a cold shower would 'straighten his head'.

11

Where. . .? Oh. Oh, yes. I think I remember. Or do I?

And, the moment after recollecting why she was in this strange shabby room that shook and trembled, Lora wished she hadn't woken up enough to do so. Her mouth tasted filthy, her stomach was sour, and there was a dull gnawing pain between her eyes.

She was stretched out naked on a hard couch covered with a sheet: old, but intact and fairly clean. It had been far too hot last night to bear any covering. It had also been too hot to go on lying next to Danty after they finished screwing. A mere touch made sweat erupt from the skin like a strike of water in a desert. So he was on the other couch, at right angles to hers.

So I finally had a black. Funny. It didn't feel any different. It was dark, of course. . .

She reached out and brushed Danty's toes with her own. His response was to bury his face deeper in his pillow.

We meant to go night-riding, didn't we? And then. . . Did he talk me out of it? I guess so, because we came here.

Not important. Not as important as the fact that her bladder was bursting. She sat up, and nearly cracked her head on a wall-hung bookcase. There were a lot of books here, she realised. On the floor, too. When she swung her legs off the couch, she trod on one and picked it up and read the title. It said: *The Calculus of Mysticism.*

Not only the books were peculiar. She saw a curious trefoil-shaped piece of plastic with furniture castors underneath, hung on string from a nail, and a plastic battery-driven orrery, one of the big ones that cost a thou-

sand bucks, and a Benham's top, and a tape-recorder
with a Buddha on the lid. The Buddha looked as though
it might be Japanese.

Hmm! So this was Danty's home! Last night she hadn't
really noticed; her attention had been elsewhere. Half
eager to relieve herself, half anxious to find out more
about him while he was asleep, she wandered the long
way around the room towards the curtain at the end
which, because it was next to an obvious shower-cabinet,
she assumed to conceal the toilet. The only other door,
apart from the entrance, was ajar and revealed a tiny kitchen.

*A violin, for goodness' sake! Or is it a viola! I wonder
if he plays it* — reaching to twang one string of it faintly
— *or if it's simply decoration.*

Curtain. She pulled it back. And discovered that it did
not give on to a toilet, but an alcove just wide enough for
a single bed, on which a dark-haired woman was asleep.

She stared for a long frozen moment. Then she let the
curtain fall and spun on her heel. Spotting her dress tossed over a chair, she ducked into it — a slow job, because
her arms kept coming out through the wrong openings.
But she managed it in the end.

Shoes? Oh, yes: left them in the car. But where the
hell had she left the car with them in?

She rushed to the window: grimy, reinforced with wire,
veiled with cheap semi-translucent curtains. Below, on the
opposite side of the street, a car that looked like hers —
the right make and model, anyway. Thank goodness.

Toilet?

The reeky turd! I'll use his shower!

She turned it on, reluctantly, when she'd finished, and
got splashed. The noise of running water aroused Danty,
and he gave her a sleepy grin and said, 'Hello, Lora.'

'Goodbye!' she snapped, and stormed out. The exit
door gave a satisfactory slam.

That was what woke Magda. When she pushed aside the curtain, she found Danty at the window, watching Lora on the way to her car. She said, 'Hi, Danty. Was it the Turpinette?'

'Hi, Magda.' He didn't look around. 'Yes.'

'Slumming, hm?' She approached and gave him a peck on a cheek stubbly with new beard.

'Yes, I guess so. And apparently regretting it this morning. But last night she had a terrific time.' He uttered a sad chuckle. 'You'll never believe this, but it's gospel. She managed to have me photographed with Prexy!'

Magda drew back half a step, staring. Abruptly she burst into helpless laughter.

'Danty! Oh, *baby!* That's the end, the ultimate end!'

'Shit, you'll be a White House consultant yet, honey,' Danty said. The car below moved off, and he turned back from the window. 'Fix some coffee, hm? I'll go take a shower. I need one. That kid has — uh — variegated tastes in BCT.'

'She doesn't call it that, does she?' Magda demanded in disbelief.

'No, she doesn't. But she confided that her mother does — or did, at least, to explain her lovers to her kids when they were young. "Body contact therapy", straight up.' He yawned and stretched. 'Tell you about it in a moment.'

By the time he was through showering and shaving, there was coffee in big mugs and Magda had put on a robe. She said as Danty sat down, 'Tell me, did it work out?'

'Yes.' Sipping his coffee, he suddenly unfocused his eyes in the disconcerting fashion he had, which made him seem to be peering into another world.

'You don't sound very happy about it.'

'Hell, no! It gets bigger and more terrifying. It's like being in a car with the governor shorted out, and some crazy fool at the wheel who wants to prove he's as good

..s a machine at a hundred-fifty. I mean — hell! I *knew* I
had to be at the scrapyard, but I didn't know why until
I saw Josh and Shark and Potatohead getting ready to
strip and kill her. So I fish her out of trouble with this
busted rifle, so she invites me to this party, so I meet this
˙˙nuck who's a house-guest of her father's. Says he's in
˙˙ber up in Manitoba. Piss on that. He can quote the
˙˙a. I heard him. Hell, I made him! And I looked around
˙˙e garage while Lora was getting out her car, and right
˙˙xt to it was her father's and I saw it before. It was the
˙˙r waiting to pick up the man from the sea.'

'You think it's Holtzer.'

'It's Holtzer, no shit.' Danty drew a deep breath; when
he let it out again she heard his teeth rattle. 'Magda, I
am goddamned scared now! I do weirder and weirder
things for subtler and subtler reasons, and I daren't not do
them, and what frightens me worst — '

He broke off. Magda reached across the table and clas-
ped his hand.

'Well, this,' he said after a pause. 'What do I do when I
reach the point where I feel what I must do, and I can't
do it, because I'm sick , or weak, or tired out? Won't
I know I'm — well — *trapped?*'

'You ever felt that's come close to happening?' Magda
asked in a commonsensical tone. Danty pondered for a
moment.

'I guess not,' he said eventually. 'I guess with luck it
may not. If I go on getting better at using the talent, I
may be able to take precautions. I could avoid exhaustion,
for instance. Illness, though. . . I don't know.'

'The way I see it,' Magda said firmly, 'is that anything
which made you sick and weak could probably screw up
the talent anyway. It uses up a hell of a lot of your energy, that's for sure. I mean, look at you! You're not just
lean, you're scrawny! I can count your ribs.'

Danty gave his body a self-conscious glance.

'I'll fix you a good big breakfast,' Magda said, rising.

72

'After that I'll have to stash you behind the curtain. I have a customer due at noon.'

'No need for that,' Danty said. 'I guess I can relax a bit today. I don't feel there's anything I have to do at once.'

He added, stretching, 'Christ! Does that make a change!'

Sunday was spreading slowly across the nation. The superways, of course, were packed to capacity — literally millions of people knew no more enjoyable way to spend their free time than hurtling from place to place at high speed. Many people routinely did a thousand miles every weekend, and a few notched up double that.

Buzzing low over one stretch of superway close to the Atlantic coast there came a flight of plain grey helicopters, their only distinguishing mark a big white number: 33. Recognising them, people in cars below began to wind down windows and wave, and probably also shout, only the traffic noise drowned out their cries.

Everyone was always delighted when they spotted one of the Energetics General service teams. More than the Army (because the Army was often called on for domestic duties and hence was little liked by those who had personal experience of martial law), and far more than the Navy (because the Navy had gone into politics full-time — the current Prexy was a Navy nominee, though likely to be the last for some time because everyone knew that Army was winding up for the next election and had something extraordinary up its collective sleeve — and most Americans still vaguely distrusted professional politicians), the engineers of EG were the people who had armed and armoured the United States against the malevolence of a hostile world.

In the lead helicopter of the flight, Gunnar Sandstrom waved back, because he knew his crew expected it of him, but he was glad when the superway was out of sight. He was becoming more and more concerned about his name. He was wondering how to change it to something — well, something *plainer*. It had been an okay thing for the past couple of decades to bear a Scandinavian patronymic, but the climate was getting tougher all the time, and you could hardly find any Polish, Italian or German names now.

On the other hand, if he did decide to indent for a fresh name, it would mean months of grilling by security, probably temporary suspension from his job, endless re-evaluation of his record, and he might all too easily be graded down to so low a clearance that EG couldn't keep him on. . .

He was still debating with himself when they came to the reserved area which was their day's destination. But he hadn't reached a decision. And he knew he would go on pondering tomorrow, the day after, the day after. . . He had been divorced once because his wife, in the long run, didn't like the name which had originally struck her as romantic. And at thirty-five it was getting harder and harder to find girls who were still inclined to regard a touch of 'foreignness' as interesting.

In accordance with normal routine, the 'copters made a pass beyond the reserved area to check the seaward side. A mile to the north there was a beach which wasn't too badly fouled with oil, sewage and garbage to be used, and now and then they found a small sailboat blown off course around here, or a swimmer — wearing rubber and a mask, naturally. Today, however, there was no one, so they circled and set down.

'Josh!' Potatohead said, and pointed at a display of papers outside the little store they were passing on the way to a hoverhalt? 'Saw'n *Cronkle?*'

'Ahsh'd lookun-at asswiper?' Josh grunted. He meant it. The *Chronicle* was a Navy paper, always carried dozens of pictures of Prexy, and admirals, and turds like that.

But fat on Sundays, lasted a whole week in a toilet.

'Na front! Seeth'addle cock 'narleq'in?'

Josh started, and bent to look at the caption. 'Shite,' he said, having painfully puzzled out the words. 'Say, she dottuv Turpin, VG! Pissun *shit*!'

Shark Bance craned over his shoulder. He read nearly as well as Josh and never missed a chance to prove it. After a moment he said, 'Hey! Week'dad ransom fo' *her*— lahk millun bucks!'

Josh gave him a wordless snarl. 'Yea! An' lookun nexter inna pic. Pegdun? Hm?'

'Sho'!' Potatohead said. 'Howsee call'?'

'Dan,' Josh worked out. 'Tee. Wah — nah, shit. *Ward.*' He straightened, and put on an evil grin. 'So, hey! Tha' blabbo dundus hurt, nah? Nextahm seeyum, weena hurtum histun!'

12

The *Chronicle*, the Navy paper; the *Bulletin*, the Army paper; the TV tuned to WSA; hangover cure, juice, coffee. . . Comforting, familiar, the landmarks which located Lewis Raymond Turpin at Sunday morning. Naturally, he had learned far more last night than he could expect to from the day's formal news. About a thousand people decided what the modern American public ought to think, and over fifty of them had been at his party. Prexy not being one, of course.

Only the second year of his term, and already the faceless mass was beginning to hear bad rumours! How much longer would Army let things ride? Would there be a coup and an impeachment, or just a diplomatic illness and voluntary relinquishment of office? (Add quotes around that word 'voluntary'.)

It would be good for Energetics General whichever way. Navy detested EG; so many of its top brass recalled the proud days of Polaris submarines. Then EG had introduced the Night-sticks, and. . .

The process had already been under way when he arrived a quarter-century ago. By then, the ten biggest corporations in the country were being sustained on taxpayers' money — aircraft, chemicals, computers, transportation services, virtually all the key industries were being regularly transfused with government funds. Naturally, because any other form of federal investment was castigated as 'creeping socialism', it had to be via the Defence Department that the money passed. A generation of ingenious public-relations work had convinced the public that this aspect of government activity was sacrosanct, never to be questioned by a loyal citizen.

The percentages crept up. Energetics General, back in those far-off days, had drawn only some eighteen per cent of its budget from the DoD. Currently the figure was closer to ninety, and since Turpin was a senior vice-president now — a mere eleven steps below the pinnacle of the EG hierarchy — the President came to his parties. So did the Chairman of the Joint Chiefs, even though he was an admiral. So did everybody who really counted.

Now suppose, just suppose, there was going to be a coup against Prexy — what they called in the history texts a 'palace revolution', because of course the faceless mass would never be allowed to learn the details. Would that bring about the long-desired collapse of this overblown, top-heavy, outright dangerous economic cancer?

He feared not. Perhaps in another decade. Right now, there were still too many clever, dedicated, and *insulted* men in positions of influence, who remembered how they had been shot at in Viet-Nam, bombed in the Philippines, and ultimately spat upon in Panama. It wasn't their fault, they maintained, that they'd been dragged home under orders to quell insurrection, and that the other side had been waiting to pounce, so that when their house was set in order they had nothing else to do but squabble for power.

There had been a great weariness, a vast sense of futility. Everything they had undertaken with the best intentions had turned sour. Like an injured porcupine, exposing its spiny back to the attacker and pressing its soft belly to the ground, the nation had abandoned its outside commitments one by one and planted automatic missile sites along its coasts. The grandiose space-programme decayed, and for fifteen years or more no American had been launched into space except to service the orbiting missile-detectors — there were thousands. Meantime, not from courtesy but a sense of self-preservation, the space-going powers duly notified every launching — for fear it might be mistaken for an attack — to the DoD.

Not to the White House. What would be the point? Effective government in America *was* the DoD.

During the four years of training which had preceded his injection into the States as man who had not previously existed, yet who sprang convincingly full-grown into a flawless background, he had been told, over and over, the orthodox analogies. Look at what happened to the Romans, they said, when internal discord prevented them from deploying their own forces to guard their frontiers. They hired barbarian mercenaries, and within a century or two those same mercenaries took over. For 'barbarian mercenaries' read 'corporations under contract to the Department of Defence', and you have it right there.

Or else: look what happened to Spain and Portugal, when they lost their empires in the New Worlds. From world-power status both countries declined into poverty, intellectual underdevelopment, and dictatorship. Or, most graphically of all, consider the British: tricked into electing a right-wing government that forcibly deported black — but not white — immigrants; expelled in consequence from their own Commonwealth of Nations, which fell apart; denied membership of the 'rich man's club' of Europe because of this incredible display of perfidy... and now moaning in squalor about the cruel way the world had treated them.

He had half expected America to collapse following the Black Exodus, six years ago, when in response to a collective invitation issued by the member-states of the OAU tens of thousands of highly skilled black intellectuals and their families had emigrated — to the accompaniment of cries of, 'Good riddance!' Unfortunately all that had accomplished was to chop off the heads of the Black Power movement, leaving an amorphous quarrelsome carcase which the government found infinitely easier to handle.

Some of those emigrants had been disillusioned. Swallowing their pride, they had applied for re-admission, and had been turned down.

'Told you so!'

So he was not very optimistic about seeing the downfall of Fortress America in his lifetime.

On the other hand. . .

From the moment of Sheklov's arrival until now, he had been so on edge about successfully cementing the newcomer's cover that he had paid little heed to the news he had brought. The notion that some alien species might trigger a nuclear holocaust was too far from his everyday preoccupations; he had been sweating and shaking and dosing himself with tranks for fear some petty error on Sheklov's part would alert the ever-watchful security force that never ceased its surveillance of Energetics General executives. Now the major obstacle was past — now that Sheklov had been photographed in company with Prexy, when everyone took it that Crashaw, Levitt and the team at their backs were the ultimate court of appeal concerning security — he could coldly review what he had been told.

Amazing. He hadn't even realised that the Russians had ventured as far as Pluto; naturally the American news media did not carry details of such achievements, and his contacts with Russian agents in Canada were sporadic and too brief for mere gossip. And they'd been out there for three years! Fantastic!

A stir of half-forgotten pride in his native land rose in the fringe of his awareness. As always, he slapped it down. For a quarter-century he had been careful to ape the opinions of those around him. He said the proper things about terrorism, bomb-outrages, insurrections, rebs, those ungrateful devils overseas. He took his vacations in the right places: at home, and usually in Florida. Before he married, he had travelled a little, but to the permissible allies, South Africa and Australia. Now and then, on business, he went to Canada — ostensibly to sound out projects which might bring in some desperately scarce foreign currency. He never enjoyed those trips, except in a an upside-down fashion. The Canadians made it plain that they too would prefer to sever relations with the States, but it was known in the way such matters are known that if they tried it they would be occupied, like Mexico; things were quiet enough at home for the troops to be spared. So they compromised by flagrantly favouring the East Bloc, and the most heavily patronised ocean cruises nowadays run by Canadian Pacific were to Vladivostok via Japan.

He had had to turn somersaults in his head now and then. When he first came to the States, he had fully expected there would be a temporary alliance between the two super-powers against China, which might degenerate into shooting war. But that had been a wrong guess. As soon as American forces began to be recalled to fight at home, it had become obvious that the Chinese were going to expand into the resulting vacuum, and unless the two schools of communism resolved their differences fast the Maoists were going to leave the Leninists standing. (What *was* the distinction between 'homoousian' and 'homoiousian'?)

Hasty conferences, a couple of treaties, the firing of a few scapegoats, and the definition of spheres of influence — not very sharply, because the parties were always jockeying for advantage — had led to the present formally courteous accommodation, which was being strengthened as in both major countries the effects of fourth- and fifth-generation commitment were felt. A little confidence in your ancestors' achievements could work wonders.

And in your own achievements, too. He'd had a bad moment yesterday evening when Lora insisted on dragging that black into the photo with Prexy. Of course, she'd done it in order to embarrass him, just as she'd put on that dress she knew he loathed. Yet, as he'd realised a second later, everyone present who had kids of the same age, including Prexy — for what he was worth — would have sympathised instead of being repelled. It was a kind of in-group status symbol nowadays for teenagers to keep up this family-scale guerrilla warfare. *Pour épater les bourgeois!* But sooner or later they'd learn that the minds of the bourgeois had been blown long before they were born.

So if anything her grand gestures, inviting this black to the party and parading around with him for hours on end, was more likely to have reinforced than weakened his cover!

Though naturally it would make sense to have security double-check the boy. . .

Now then: what about this question of the alien ship? What did they imagine, Back There, that he could *do*? He'd made all the suggestions to Sheklov which he could think of on the spur of the moment: financing some sort of hypothetical study of the problem, for example, under the guise of training in management initiative, along the lines of courses he'd heard of many years ago which were given to industrial designers. You invented an imaginary race with three legs, or sonar instead of eyes, or living underwater, and told the students to equip this species with transport and accommodation. But this, although he personally regarded it as an inspiration because it was perfectly feasible to ask some bright young people, 'How do we trade with contraterrene creatures?', apparently meant nothing to Sheklov. He kept talking about 'an attitude of mind'.

Have to go over this again in detail. Say after lunch in the den. Give the room another sweep for bugs first, naturally. But right now. . .

Pressure which had been building up in his bladder since he awoke finally drove Turpin out of bed.

13

There appeared to be a ritual about Sunday in the Turpin household. Sheklov hoped fervently that he wouldn't have to endure it more than once. But apparently Mrs Turpin's mother insisted on it. Her name was Gleewood, but that had not been the maiden name of Mrs Turpin. There had been some divorces — a fact which did not in the least surprise him.

Not wishing to seem discourteous, he accepted Mrs Gleewood's invitation to join her and her daughter in the livingroom and watch Reverend Powell's nationally-networked service at noon — the 'lip service', as someone had caustically termed it during last night's party. Peter, looking haggard, came too, several minutes after it started. That triggered off a lecture from his grandmother concerning the disgracefully casual attitude of young people to religion. Then she asked where Lora was, and Peter answered sharply, "Lying on her bed in a drunken stupor — where else?"

Which gave an excuse for another and longer blast. Sheklov sat there wishing the floor would open and swallow him, while Mrs Turpin — Sophie, as she insisted he call her — simply sat with glacial calmness, sipping a rapid succession of gin atomics brought by Estelle. To reinforce his cover, Sheklov had intended to talk a little with the maid in the family's hearing about their supposedly shared homeland; so far, however, the girl had absolutely refused to be drawn.

It had crossed his mind, very vaguely, that she might not be Canadian herself, but the only reason he could

82

think of for pretending to be was if she was wanted for a
criminal offence, and had changed her identity to one
which could not be too closely investigated. The
Canadians were efficiently unco-operative when it came
to answering inquiries from the States about their citizens.

Still, that was irrelevant. Right now, his job was to
put himself beyond the reach of unwelcome prying.

To start with, he must get Turpin to have this Danty
checked out. Turpin would have an excellent excuse to
do so, considering his daughter's connection with the
boy. Boy? More like young man. Over twenty, under
twenty-five. Hard to be sure owing to his bony leanness.

Had it surprised him to find that a Canadian timber-
salesman could quote the *Bhagavad-Gita?* He hadn't
shown the least hint of it, just given a nod of satisfaction
at the aptness of the passage. True, one did find people
who adhered to non-western religions both here and
north of the border. But it was so atypical, he shivered
imperceptibly whenever he recalled his incredible lapse.
He had *had* to utter those words. It was as though someone else took momentary command of his tongue.

Then there was lunch, at which Turpin appeared with
a sort of after-shave advertisement bluffness and a forced
air of goodwill towards the world, and — shortly after —
Lora too, tousle-haired, bleary-eyed, and even more
snappish than Peter. Mrs Gleewood told her what she
thought of her behaviour, in particular because she had
dared to bring a black into her own home, when everybody knew that all the blacks in America were ready to
slip a knife in your ribs the instant they got the chance.

'Don't talk to me about that radiated slug,' was Lora's
sullen answer, at which Mrs Gleewood rounded on
Turpin.

'You know what this rude little bitch needs?' she
rasped. 'Six months in a reform camp, that's what!'

'Hear, hear!' — loudly from Peter.

Details about reform camps had been included in Sheklov's briefing. He expected Turpin to explode at that. The camps were for incorrigible juvenile delinquents, and the most famous — at Sandstone, Georgia — boasted the highest murder-rate and the highest suicide-rate in the country. But Turpin merely said in a mild tone, 'Lora will get over this phase, you know.'

'The hell I will,' Lora said, and moodily turned to her food.

By the time Turpin suggested he and Sheklov adjourn to the room he called his den, for coffee and liqueurs, it was all the latter could do not to shake his head in inexpressible admiration. Coping with this abominable mother-in-law, this near-alcoholic wife, this homosexual son, this promiscuous daughter, and his job at Energetics General *and* his rôle as the best Russian agent ever to be injected into the States — it defied belief!

When Turpin had assured him that the den was clean of bugs and they could talk freely, he tried to say something of what he was feeling. But Turpin, pouring tiny goblets of Tia Maria, stared in apparently genuine incomprehension.

'Don, I don't see what you mean. Sure, the kids are a bit wild, but I meant it when I said they'd settle down. Granted, I'm sort of sorry about Peter, but it's this protracted-adolescence bit, and it's simply the — uh — the in-thing to flaunt your defiance of the conventions for a few years before you straighten your head and cool off. He has girls too, you know, now and then.'

'Nonetheless, a family like this must be — '

'My family,' Turpin cut in with an air of not wanting to be contradicted, 'is my best single cover. Sophie is a first-rate company wife. If it hadn't been for her, I could never have got where I am. I have to endure her mother, of course, but we only see her during the summer; she has a winter place in Florida. I planned the family to *be* my cover, in fact, so if you have any quarrel with it, you go blame the census department. I have an average number of kids, I give them average allowances, they've had typical educations, typical everything. My only worry has been that sometimes I've wondered whether someone might not figure it was so close to the norm it must be planned.'

He hesitated, and then added, 'My only worry, that is, until you were wished on me. Are you making any progress?' And added with his eyes: *I hope!*

Sheklov reached for the bowl of sugar resting on a low table between them and stirred a generous spoonful into his coffee; he liked it Turkish-style, thick and sweet. Not looking up, he said, 'I'm not a miracle-worker, you know. I shall have to feel things out for a good while before I can do anything positive.'

Turpin sighed. 'I don't see why someone had to be sent specially,' he grumbled. 'Or why — if it was necessary — it had to be me who was used to cushion you.'

'Also,' Sheklov said delicately, 'you don't like the scope of my brief.'

There was a pause. Turpin looked everywhere except at Sheklov while deciding how best to reply. He settled for candour. 'No, I don't!'

'If it's any consolation, it makes me feel awkward, too,' Sheklov raised his liqueur goblet. Barely in time he remembered to sip, not toss the contents back. While thinking as Holtzer he made no such errors, he reassured himself; it was trying to straddle his two personalities which —

But that led back to the recollection of how he had exposed himself to Danty.

Maintaining flawless outward calm, however, he said, 'In fact, I was going to ask you this anyhow, and now is as good a time as any. How long would it take you to fix me a job with EG — a travelling job?'

Turpin's face went turkey-cock red. He said, 'Now just a—!

85

'I have the authority to insist,' Sheklov murmured.

'The hell you do! Look, they gave me to understand that your timber-salesman cover was fireproof, that the parent firm has been used before and can prop you up as long as necessary!'

'As long as necessary for me to devise an alternative,' Sheklov answered stonily. 'You know as well as I do — I mean *better* than I do — that even a Canadian isn't allowed to stay in this country without impeccable reasons.'

Turpin's jowls trembled. 'But they told me I only had to cushion your landfall. I took it for granted that you had a closed assignment!'

'Nobody said that in so many words,' Sheklov pointed out. 'In fact my assignment is open-ended, category one. Anyway, why should the idea of finding me a job with EG upset you so much? You must be distributing patronage all the time.'

'Patronage!' Turpin echoed, and slapped his thigh with his open palm, like a gun-shot. 'This isn't patronage — it's blackmail! Bringing you into EG would be insanely dangerous. I've sweated blood for years, for decades, to make sure there was no one in the entire corporation who had a breadth of suspicion against him. I'm damned if I'm going to break a clean record a quarter-century long!'

Eventually Sheklov sighed and turned around in his chair to a more comfortable position.

'Look, Dick,' he said, 'there's something that doesn't seem to have registered with you yet. Out near Pluto something has happened which is so big that nothing else matters until it's resolved. Doesn't that get across to you? Hell, there *are* alien intelligences! There *are* portions of the universe which are contraterrene! And because one damned idiot government out of all the damned idiot governments we have on this miserable planet has signed away its responsibility to a bunch of machines, you and

I and everybody, communist or capitalist, neutralist or whatever the hell, *all* of us, could be hurled back to the Stone Age tomorrow — if we're still alive. Think about it, Dick, for pity's sake *think*!'

It was getting through. He could read it in Turpin's staring eyes. He had finally managed to smash down the mental barriers in the other's head. And by doing so, inevitably, he had brought the whole affair back into focus in his own consciousness with as much force as it had possessed when he first heard of it from Bratcheslavsky in Alma-Ata.

At that moment, though, a phone shrilled. Turpin snatched at it. It was one of the old-fashioned kind that had to be held to the ear; in that case, Sheklov reasoned, it was probably a confidential line. Modern designs were easier to bug.

'Turpin here!'

There was a crackling. He nodded. 'Yes, this is my quiet line. You can talk.'

The caller talked. Watching, Sheklov saw Turpin's face go pasty-grey; his eyes narrowed, and he closed his empty fist so tight the knuckles glistened white. He look-as though he was about to swing that fist in sheer fury.

'Yes, I'll come at once,' he said thickly when the caller was through. He slammed down the phone, leaped from his chair, and towered over Sheklov.

'You turd!' he forced out. 'You radiated bastard!'

'What happened?' Sheklov whispered, thinking of Danty.

'That reserved area where you came ashore! They sent a service crew there today. Know what they found? They found it had been *turned off* in the small hours of the morning you arrived. Turned off! Do you understand what that means?'

Sheklov did. But waited for Turpin to put it into smoking words.

'It means someone else knows you're here,' Turpin

spat. 'And you've put both our necks in a noose!'

14

Around the shoulder of the world, Bratcheslavsky had once said without warning, in the middle of a training session, 'Vassily Sheklov!'

To which he had reacted with a surprised cock of his eyebrows.

'Know why you've been picked for this assignment?'

'Well.' Selecting the least arrogant-seeming of a dozen possible answers in the space of less than a heartbeat, and moreover not wanting to appear to cast doubt on the competence of those who had singled him out by adopting a pose of exaggerated modesty. 'Well, because out of the range available, I guess I must be the most suitable. . . comrade.'

'Your diplomatic turns of phrase do you credit,' Bratcheslavsky chuckled, stubbing the latest of the aromatic cigarettes which were certain to kill him before his time. 'But *I'm* not here to have my perspicacity flattered, regardless of what you may safely put over on other people. I guess it hasn't escaped your notice that one of the luxuries America permits itself is an exceptional degree of subtlety in the shades of meaning conveyed by the English language?'

At which: a nod.

'Well, then. During your long struggle with the various idioms of modern English, you can hardly have failed to run across the image of someone "thinking fast on his feet" — hm?'

'Of course, comrade. A metaphor drawn from boxing, I believe. A term of praise for someone who — '

'Boxing be buggered,' Bratcheslavsky retorted. They were speaking English, of course; the entire briefing was conducted in it, the ideal being to drive Russian so far to the fringes of Sheklov's consciousness that he would not be recognised as a Russian-speaker by those who might survey him after his injection into the States. 'The idiom is used by people who hate boxing, who wouldn't pay ten cents to get into a boxing-match, who would call up and complain if a TV company wasted programme-time on an international championship! No, the image is detached from its origins. And what I want to know is this: do you recognise its applicability to this mission?'

'You mean it was a quality which was taken into consideration when they picked me for it.'

'*The* quality, Vassily. The most important of all. Were it not for your possession of this talent, we might well have given up all hope of injecting another agent as blatantly as we shall have to in your case. Human beings have this peculiar limitation on their thinking, you know: they tend to put up with enormous risks simply because they can't exhaustively analyse the nature of the actions they realise they ought to take to insure themselves. As thinkers, Vassily, we are an amazingly lazy species. It's a wonder we survive from one day to the next. Yes! Let's get on with it!'

All of which sprang back instantly into Sheklov's mind, vivid as a 3D movie picture.

He said coldly to Turpin, still looming over him as though about to tear him limb from limb, 'Shut up and sit down.'

'You — !'

'I said shut up!' With an access of unfeigned anger. 'I wish you'd use your wits now and then! You just said someone else must have known I was coming ashore, didn't you? But you didn't take one deep breath and ask yourself who! Put your vanity away, will you?'

90

'What?' But his anger was turning to bluster, and Sheklov knew it.

'You heard. Stop and think for a moment. *Who* would be in a position to know that something was going to happen offshore at a reserved area? Do you imagine you're unique?'

Slowly Turpin sank back into his chair. 'I — I don't follow you.'

'That's obvious.' Sheklov loaded his tone with sarcasm. 'I'll spell it out, then. You claim your cover has never been penetrated, right?'

'Of course! You think they'd let someone in my position ride for twenty-five years? Hell, no!'

'If that's true of you, it may be true of someone else.'

'You mean someone I don't know about was instructed to make sure I did cushion your landfall? I — '

'No! To make sure the submarine wasn't shot out of the water.'

'Then why was he crazy enough to leave the site shut down, knowing that next time a service crew came by security forces would flock after them like — like crows?' Turpin produced a small phial from his pocket, shook out a white tablet, and gulped it down with a swig of now-cold coffee. Sheklov seized the chance to thrust a fresh proposal home.

'Then look at it this way. Is it easy to shut down one of your sites?'

'Easy?' Turpin echoed with an incredulous laugh. 'Hell, no. I could just about shut one down from memory, but I'd rather have a schematic in front of me. You have to close nine of a series of twelve switches in a special order — that's after you get through a sintered-ceramic door — and the other three are dummies wired straight into Continental Defence HQ!'

'In other words,' Sheklov said, leaning forward, 'who-ever did this had access to confidential EG data. Suppose this had nothing to do with me. Suppose it was aimed at

91

Energetics General. What about your rival corporations? Aren't some of them resentful of EG's exclusive contract for automatic defence systems?'

'Well. . . ' The trank Turpin had swallowed was taking effect; he was able to consider the notion calmly.

'Come to that,' Sheklov pressed, 'the Navy isn't too happy about the situation, I'm told.'

'My God,' Turpin said slowly.

'You see my point? Suppose one of EG's staff has been bribed to demonstrate that your systems are vulnerable to sabotage!'

Turpin sat stock-still for long seconds. Abruptly he jumped to his feet. 'It's thin! Christ, it's thin! But you're right — it could be a way to misdirect the investigation. I'll shoot for it. But it's going to be hell anyhow. Because . . . Well, you know the only way to break EG's contract on this?'

Sheklov shook his head.

'To impeach the Board for treason. In which case I can confidently expect to be shot to death by an Army firing squad. And I couldn't help but take you with me. They have very efficient interrogation-drugs nowadays.'

He glanced at his watch, and concluded, 'I must go. They said they'd have a veetol on the beach for me in ten minutes.'

The moment the door closed, Sheklov's self-control failed and he began to shake. His mouth dried, his guts churned, and for a terrible few seconds he thought his bladder was going to let go. Just in time, he forced a deep breath into his lungs, and held it, and was able to deploy the resources due to his yoga training: the *pranayana* first, to cancel out the panic-reactions of his body, and then a series of mental exercises to drive unrealised possibilities back to their proper status in his awareness.

But the shock had reached deep down through his personality, to layers which had already been badly bruised by his encounter with Danty, and it was a long process. It was still not complete when he realised with a start that someone else was in the room: Lora.

'I'm sorry,' she muttered from the doorway. 'But I heard Dad go out, and I thought maybe I could sneak in here and get away from everybody. But if you don't want to be disturbed — '

With an effort Sheklov put back his Holtzer mask, and smiled at her.

'Come in by all means. I can't — well, I guess this isn't the thing for a guest to say, but I can't blame you for wanting to hide out for a bit.'

Gratefully she shut the door and came to sit in the chair her father had been using. She dropped into it like a limp doll, legs sprawled, and he realised with a shock that she was wearing nothing under her short black indoor robe. During lunch he hadn't noticed; so much of her had been hidden under the table.

Obviously, though, it hadn't occurred to her that exposing her crotch was either immodest or discourteous. He considered, very briefly, reverting to the full Holtzer pattern and commenting in shocked terms, then decided he should risk not doing so to secure an opening for some inquiries about Danty.

While he was casting around for the correct turn of phrase to lead into the subject, however, she saved him the trouble. 'Don, what do you think of Danty?' she demanded suddenly.

'Ah. . . ' *Careful!* 'As a matter of fact, I found him quite an interesting young man. I was astonished when he claimed to be a reb, because he's not at all what you'd imagine. I got the idea he was putting people on.'

'You mean like needling Reverend Powell?'

'Oh, that — yes! I've seen Powell on TV now and then, of course, but last night was the first time I'd met him. And I was not impressed.' *Good; that came out in the proper tone of stuffy disapproval.*

'Exactly right for Peter,' Lora muttered. 'Christ, they make a lovely pair. . . Say, Don — ! Oh, never mind.'

'What?'

She made a vague gesture, staring disconsolately at her delicately-fingered hands. 'Oh. . . Oh, I was just going to ask if you'd like to sleep with me for the rest of your stay. So I could get out of Peter's company. I think you're nice. You smile a lot, as though you mean it, and somewhere underneath there's something — well — something real about you. If you see what I mean. So I just thought. . .'

Another gesture like the former.

Startled, Sheklov said after a pause, 'Well, I'm flattered — I guess. But. . . Well, your parents, for one thing. . .' The words tailed away.

Flattered isn't it. I'm flabbergasted!

'Oh, them!' Lora said. 'Think they give a fart what I do? They never have done. That's why I do all these crazy things. They call it 'tolerance', or 'freedom from inhibitions', or some shit like that. What it means really is, they have an excuse for not bothering about their kids. . . Still, I guess it might foul up your business deal with Dad, hm?'

'Well — uh — it might,' Sheklov said. 'And in any case you won't have to share with Peter much longer. I expect to leave in a day or two. And if you'll forgive my saying so, I had the impression you're involved with Danty.'

'Oh, I'm such a reeky fool!' Her eyes were staring into infinity. 'I got so mad this morning, over at his place. About something that doesn't matter at all. I mean, I've done much worse things to people — do them all the time. I think sometimes I'll go crazy, right out of my skull crazy. Maybe cut my throat in a fit of the blues.'

She sounded as though she meant it. Sheklov's spine crawled.

'Well, surely you haven't done anything you can't put right by apologising,' Sheklov ventured. 'I certainly hope you didn't. Like I said, I found Danty kind of interesting, and I hoped I might see him again, talk some more.'

'Really?' She sat up sharply and her eyes lost their glazed look.

'Why not? You know, I must admit I don't like this attitude you find down here, about young people — as though they had to be sort of quarantined. Hell, I'm not so old myself, I'm thirty-five, and back home I have friends from — '

But she wasn't listening. 'You mean if I went looking for him I could — well, I could say you wanted me to, not just have to crawl to him and eat dirt?' She jumped to her feet.

'If that would help, sure you can.' And Sheklov thought: *I'm going to be a long time figuring out the mores here!*

'Oh, Don!' Lora exclaimed, clasping her hands. 'I love you!'

She rushed forward, jumped on his lap, and thrust her tongue into his mouth.

15

The melodramatic — yet in a sense very real — self-directed threat he had uttered to Sheklov had had a curious stabilising effect on Turpin's mind. It couldn't just be the tranquilliser; during his twenty-five-year balancing act, he had faced all kinds of crises from the risk of divorce to full-scale investigations of Energetics General by a House committee, and he had relied on drugs time and again to tide him over. He knew what they could and couldn't do.

This state of mind was unique — a sensation as though a shaft of ice had been thrust clear from his crown to the base of his spine.

And the chill seemed to pervade every nook and cranny of his being. Ordinarily, while a veetol was hovering on its jets waiting for clearance into a traffic-lane, he was a trifle scared — particularly when, as now, there was deep water underneath.

Today, though, the notion of having a thousand feet of nothing between him and disaster didn't trouble him in the least. It was almost enjoyable. He had discovered a sort of pride in his own resilience. He knew better than to surrender to it — pride could be as dangerous as panic — but Sheklov had convinced him that exposure was far from unavoidable after all. (*Damn the man!* his subconscious added silently. *Sabotage by the Navy, or another company, should have occurred to me, not to him!*)

The situation was bad. It didn't have to be irremediable. It had better not be.

He had left Russia too soon to learn the same yoga techniques as Sheklov — they had not been adopted until long after his injection into the States — but trial and error had taught him what he needed to think of in order to calm his mind. He concentrated now on the crucial factors, re-calling his own earlier recognition of the value of having confidence in one's achievements. Sheklov had told him, more than once since his arrival, that he was still regarded as the most valuable agent ever planted on this continent — and wasn't there truth in that compliment? His position as a senior vice-president of EG was virtually impregnable. Energetics General, in most people's minds, was synonymous with the sacred concept of continental defence, and he was looked up to by everyone he came in contact with — even by Prexy's backers, despite their being Navy.

Prexy himself as well, of course — but he didn't count for a fart in a bath-tub.

He slacked the buckles of his seat-harness a little as his confidence grew and grew. Yes, he could believe that Sheklov had been sent to him because his cover was perfect. And they did still set store by him Back There. They must. For the good and sufficient reason that he was the one who had coped. He was the one who had remained afloat when so many others had sunk — been tried and executed, or in a few cases which rankled in his memory killed by a mob, during the bad period of the late seventies when a single month might see as many as two thousand lynchings of political suspects, drug-users, and young men with long hair or beards.

He was in an almost benevolent mood when the reserved area hove in sight and the pilot called, 'Mr Turpin! We're going in for a landing now — please tighten your harness.'

He was delighted to see how steady his hands were as he gripped the straps.

From the nearby superway it would have been impossible to tell that anything out of the ordinary was occur-
ring in the reserved area. Stands of trees forced with
paragibberellins and a rise in the ground concealed the
immensely powerful four-engined helicopters which had
brought the service crew. Turpin caught only a brief
glimpse of them as his pilot — properly conscious of not
having a high enough clearance to enter a reserved area —
set down a couple of minutes' walk away. He noticed that
their sides were branded with the white figures '33', and
tried to recollect more about the members of this team
than simply their names.

Hurrying towards them, he saw that around the nearest
'copter several men in the quasi-military uniform of
fatigues and technical harness (which, he recalled not
without pride, he had been instrumental in having
adopted to emphasise the dedicated rôle these men played
in Continental Defence) were milling like ants. With one
foot on the ground, the other on the ledge of the
'copter's door, a blond man in his middle thirties was
shooting questions by turns at each of his engineers.
Turpin knew him instantly, although he had only met
him once or twice, and months ago. That was the crew-
boss, Gunnar Sandstrom, about whom security had been
so dubious when his appointment came up. Because of
the behaviour of the Scandinavian governments, of
course, who refused to hand over traitors and deserters.

He had just started to call and wave to attract Sandstrom's attention when the howl of another aircraft
battered their ears, rising in the blink of an eye from a
drone to an intolerable roar. The shadow of it flickered
over Turpin a fraction of a second before the noise hit;
reflexively he glanced up at the bright sky, and was
blinded — in his haste to leave home, he had forgotten
his dark glasses. But he caught a glimpse of its white
paint-job, nonetheless, and cursed silently. He had hoped
to be here before any of the senior security people

showed, to plant his suspicions about inter-corporation sabotage.

Too late now, though. Somebody very top indeed had arrived. That was no ordinary veetol, but a Mach Three type, capable of crossing the continent in barely more than an hour.

Its pilot — if it was piloted, and not automatically controlled — set it down with meticulous accuracy in the middle of the cluster of choppers. Almost before the power had been cut its door was thrown open and a heavy-set man with black hair, wearing a bright blue windbreaker and orange pants, jumped to the ground. Sandstrom, naturally, broke off his conversation with his engineers and went running to meet him.

Turpin felt a brief pang of dismay. This was someone he didn't recognise. He'd hoped at least that they would send an acquaintance of his, sympathetic to EG. Still, there was no alternative to putting a bold face on the matter. He too strode up to the newcomer, as he was checking Sandstrom's redbook.

'Good morning! Or rather, good afternoon!' he said. 'I'm Turpin of Energetics General. I left home as soon as I heard what had happened.' He offered his hand.

The black-haired man looked at it for a while, not moving to take it, and then raised piercing eyes to Turpin's face.

'Redbook?' he murmured.

Almost, Turpin let it be seen how insulted he felt, but he recovered in time and meekly produced the document — adding, as he handed it over, 'Good afternoon to you too, Gunnar. Walked into a hornet's nest, didn't you?'

The crew-boss, looking troubled, didn't answer.

'Right,' the dark-haired man said, handing Turpin's redbook back. 'I'm — '

Turpin interrupted. 'Yours too, *please!*'

They locked gazes for a moment. Then the newcomer chuckled and reached towards his hip pocket.

'Yes, by all means, Mr Turpin. Correct procedure — oh, *shit!*'

As he touched his pocket, a yammering alarm had gone off.

He did something under his sweat-patched left armpit, and the row stopped, and he finally produced the red-book. 'Sorry,' he muttered with some embarrassment. 'New model alarm. Very efficient. But in the heat of the moment. . .'

The words tailed away.

Pleased to have rattled the security man, Turpin opened the redbook. Even before he read the first page, he had a strong idea of what he was going to find. Only the handful of key personnel who master-minded security throughout the States had those personalised alarm-systems in their clothes. Nonetheless what he discovered amazed him. Apart from redbook #000 000 001, which was allotted to Prexy, he had never seen such comprehensive clearances. 'Morton Kendall Clarke,' he read. 'Substantive bailiff, acting warden, United States Security Force. Seconded Continental Defence HQ.'

Then: five pages of departmental stamps, four of special authorisations enabling him to assume command of army, navy, police and National Guard detachments in emergency; the usual warning to the civil population that resisting his orders carried a term of not less than one year's jail. . .

It was too much. He slapped it shut and gave it back. Clarke tucked it away with a self-conscious grin, as though all too aware of how it must have affected Turpin.

'Right!' he said, turning to Sandstrom. 'Let's have the details again from the top.'

Sandstrom glanced at Turpin, but all the latter could do was nod. You didn't argue with a redbook like Clarke's. The crew-boss began to recite in a manner as impersonal as a machine.

'We set down here at fourteen-oh-three. Random-

100

schedule maintenance assignment serial·H-506-oblique-828-oblique-97. I deployed my crew in the prescribed manner. My aide, Leo Wilkie over there' — he pointed at a freckle-faced young man with a shock of tow-coloured hair — 'set about deploying the status-check gear for use when the site had been pronounced A-OK. Immediately he fired up the lice-counter, he drew my attention to. . .' He interrupted himself. 'Uh — sorry. I mean the live-circuit remote-condition reader.'

'I know what you mean,' Clarke snapped. 'Go on.'

'Yes, sure.' Sandstrom licked his lips. 'Well, right away we both realised something was wrong. Should have been displaying the regular pattern bright as day. And the screen stayed dead. I knew there wasn't a fault in the unit because it came fresh from overhaul this morning.'

'So what did you do then?'

'Sounded the recall siren and told the crewmen what I suspected. And Leo exchanged their routine gear for — uh — the appropriate equipment. In fact, by that time one of the crews, making for the master switching bunker, had had their own suspicions aroused. The locks on the bunker door were not at their former setting. The door is four-inch sintered-ceramic, a kind of artificial ruby, with. . . But I guess you've been to lots of these sites.'

'Yes,' Clarke said. 'So? What next?'

'I ordered a top-to-bottom check of the site. Didn't want to risk the chance that we'd been issued with data which actually related to somewhere else.'

'Has that ever happened to you?'

'No, sir, never. But we were warned in training not to proceed if it did happen.'

'I see. Go on.'

'Well' — Sandstrom made a helpless gesture — 'we satisfied ourselves the site really was shut down. So I sent out the alarm.'

'When?'

'I logged that, sir,' the freckle-faced Leo broke in.

'Fifty-three minutes after we landed.'

'Fifty-three minutes!' Clarke exploded. 'Nearly an hour! And now. . . ' He checked his watch. 'Now it's an hour and a half later still! What the hell were you doing all that time?'

Listening, Turpin recognised the faint whine that sharpened his voice, and shivered. He knew many people like this, more women than men but plenty of men too, who had let petty power go to their heads and enjoyed stamping on the least suggestion of dilatoriness or incompetence among their subordinates. . . and were always full of excuses for their own shortcomings. He knew, and suspected that Clarke knew too, that checking out a site of this complexity in an hour was fast work.

Unfortunately, of course, when it comes to someone who holds a redbook like Clarke's, you can't talk about 'petty' power. . .

Sandstrom had stiffened, his mouth tensing as though he wanted to snap back but dared not. He said in a dead tone, 'What I was doing, *sir*, was acting in accordance with my instruction manual. That's to say, evaluating the status of every potentially deadly item of equipment in the reserved area in order to protect my crewmen from accidental injury. If that's a satisfactory answer, I'll proceed to what I did after sending out the alarm.'

'So tell me,' Clarke said with a scowl.

'I deployed half my men along the beach, under orders to look for any sign of someone coming from the sea who might have sabotaged the installation. And I deployed the other half into the woods and along the track leading to the superway, with the same — '

'Gunnar!' A top-of-the-lungs shout. They spun around. On the dirt road leading towards this spot, a man running and calling and waving, obviously very agitated. 'Gunnar, this way, quick!'

And, a couple of minutes later, Turpin, Clarke, Sand-

102

strom and two members of the maintenance crew were staring down at a footprint on the side of a now-dry puddle — or rather, at half a footprint. Only the sole had left a mark. But that was clear enough for the brand-name to be read.

16

Well ahead of the scheduled time of Magda's meet with her client, Danty had left the apartment, revelling in the sensation of not being driven to do things whose outcome he could not foresee. He had sometimes tried to describe his — his. . . No, the word didn't exist. Say 'premonitions'? That was absolutely wrong. 'Previsions?' Wrong again. Fits of clairvoyance, perhaps. . .

Anyway: he had tried to describe them, and failed. They were an abstract, like hunger and thirst, and could only be assuaged by letting himself drift until he found the proper course of action, and pursued it. Occasionally there was a tingling or throbbing at the back of his head.

Today, however, he was luxuriously able to relax. He enjoyed that so much that for well over two hours he simply wandered about the city, saying hello now and then to his acquaintances. He had very few friends, and no close ones except Magda.

Eventually, however, he spotted a family climbing towards a hoverhalt carrying beach-gear, off for a swim, and decided on the spur of the moment to join them. The shore would be crowded, of course; today was dry and clear and not unbearably hot. Here on the Cowville side the sand was not as carefully cleansed as over by the towers of Lakonia — still, by current standards, New Lake was outstanding. Few people cared to go to the ocean any more, even if they lived within easy reach. The water was too foul. And as for rivers. . .

But in New Lake you could swim without risking instant diarrhoea and pharyngitis, and half a mile from shore you could climb on to a bobbing plastic platform and stare at Lakonia and daydream. Even blacks could daydream.

Besides, they could scoff at cocks who were due for overnight agony and lobster-redness in the morning.

When he scrambled down from the hoverhalt by the lake, one among a hundred all with the same idea, he headed straight for a rental booth where two dollars obtained you a towel. That was all you had to have. Some fine Sundays they rented five thousand towels. Judging by the length of the line ahead of him, today might top the previous high.

But before he came within ten places of the head of the line, a familiar tingling started at his nape, and slowly spread.

Oh, no! he pleaded silently, and stood fast, trying to disregard it.

Eventually, however, it reached the point where — he knew from experience — he had to respond, or suffer night after night of sleepless worrying, guessing at answers for the question which could never be answered: 'Suppose I had. . . ?'

Furious, within a minute of reaching the rental booth, he broke out of the line and stared wildly about him. No one paid much attention to his behaviour, except the girl behind him, who was so eager to get in the water she was undressing already. You got these crazy screwheads by the beach all the time.

He had very little money on him, as usual. He seldom carried more than twenty dollars, enough for car-fare and public toilets. One of the advantages of the beach was that it passed a whole day for next to nothing.

Yet his attention fixed abruptly on something he would never ordinarily have bothered with: a telescope, on a block of concrete overlooking the lake, with an engraved map of the Lakonia towers beside it — out of date by three building-projects — and the usual time-switched coin-machine controlling its shutter.

Yes. That. But why in the name of. . . ?

He sighed and walked towards it. Now, a few people did glance at him, puzzled. When money was so scarce, why waste it on peering through a telescope?

He agreed. He agreed entirely. Nonetheless he pushed his dollar into the slot and closed his eyes, *feeling* without reference to the map where he ought to point the 'scope. At once a dozen naked kids, of both sexes, who had doubtless failed to persuade their parents to give them money for the same thing, came rushing to beg a brief glimpse of Lakonia.

He ignored them, even though they tugged at his pants so hard they threatened to pull them down. It wouldn't have bothered anyone but him if they'd made it, of course; his balls weren't anything special to look at.

He re-opened his eyes just as the corroded and badly-serviced timing device on the shutter consented to admit that his coin was valid. It sprang aside — not all the way, but far enough. A three-quarter circle of brilliant sun-drenched sand appeared, backed by the colourful Lakonia towers. On the sand a veetol was standing, dwarfed by the buildings beyond, and its bright blue paint was marked with the symbol of Energetics General, a stylised star transfixed by a lightning bolt.

A man approached it at a stumbling run, mopping his forehead as he went. He looked familiar. But for an agonising instant Danty thought the handkerchief he was using would prevent a clear sight of his face. Then, though, he shoved it in his pocket as he made to climb the veetol's steps.

Christ! Turpin!

Almost before its door was shut, the veetol howled heavenwards, and Danty turned away from the 'scope to the amazement of the children around him, who took a full ten seconds before they started quarrelling over

who should make first use of the time bought and not
expended.

'Reeky pigs,' Potatohead said as he drew on his pants
— but not too loudly. The pig who had told them to quit
the beach was still within earshot. And gunshot.

'Mm-hm,' Shark said, squatting on the sand to empty
some of it out of his shoes. 'Funky traitors.'

The pig happened to be about the same colour as they
were.

'Whother fart youter do'un?' Josh said, coming back
from an ice-cream concession holding three overbalancing
cones of pale blue, yellow and pink.

'Nosser much wha'we doon,' Potatohead grunted.
'Mo' whother 'adiated cop think we shudna!'

Josh stared at them for a moment. Then, in a gesture
of all-embracing disgust, he hurled the ice-creams to the
ground and stamped on them. Nearby, a child who had
been watching with large envious eyes broke into a howl
of misery and would have charged up and pummelled
Josh but that his father seized him by the ankle and
tripped him — which led to still louder howls.

'Chrahssek!' Josh blasted. 'Youter doan' spen'nough
tahm uppie chothers' cricks? Lahk youer hanna blow,
hunh? 'Zat it?'

'We-yull. . . ' Potatohead shuffled from one foot to the
other, reincarnating Uncle Tom to the life.

'Ah, y'make muh wan' thro-*wup*!' Josh snarled.
'Y'*knoh* they dullet'nyun bu' gulls scroona beach! Fay-
yud! Mekun fast! Ah dwonna knoh youter blabbohs
'fo' y'eads get stray-yut! Heah muh? Ah s'd fay-yud!'

Briefly, Shark looked as though he might hurl himself at Josh; the latter, though, kicked with bare toes at
the pants he had left folded on the sand and parted folds
of cloth to reveal the handle of his knife. He was very
fast with it, much faster than his buddies — which was a
good reason for him to give the orders.

'Ah, piss'nya!' Shark sighed at length, and turned away.

Turpin getting into a company veetol at a run — and on a Sunday afternoon! Head down, strolling randomly along the beach and attracting cat-calls on every side, not only from girls, proposing reasons why he should have his pants on — mostly connected with needing a magnifying-glass — Danty struggled to make sense of the situation.

If it did have anything to do with him, and past experience indicated that he wouldn't have *felt* it if it didn't, then it must connect up by way of the reserved area which he'd left turned off. Why? *Why?* That was the best possible guarantee that the security force would come running!

Of course, no one would be able to link him person-ally with what he'd done. Before leaving, he had meticu-lously wiped everything he recalled touching, and his memory was good. The rock he'd hidden beside was be-low the tide-mark, and he'd gone to it over firm dry ground patched with dunegrass, so —

He stopped dead. Just ahead of him, some tender-foot had stepped in a patch of damp sand, and the mark of a plastic sandal stood out as clear as a plaster-of-Paris cast. And he remembered.

That puddle, where he'd collected mud to smear on his face! He'd seen — and he'd done nothing about — that print he'd left on its edge. . . and since Friday morning there had been no more rain!

'Josh!'

'Ah, shit! Wh'n Ah sa' fay-yud, Ah mean fay-yud!' Josh sat up, hand snaking towards his pants and the hilt of his knife.

'Nah, coolun!' Shark insisted. 'Tha' slug dun-s'all wrong — tha' Dan'y Wohd!'

Instantly Josh forgot everything else. He turned very slowly to face them, eyes blank behind his dark glasses.

108

'Sawun?'

'Sho'! Raht hyah onna *be*-yutch!'

There was a pause full of the cries of kids playing ball. At length Josh nodded and began to pull on his clothes.

'Sho'un way, hm?' he said. 'We got sco' t'level wi-yat mother.'

17

A few minutes after the discovery of the footprint, a second security veetol dropped out of the sky — not such a fast model as Clarke's, but much larger, bringing a top forensic team with all their gear. Under Clarke's direction they set about turning the site inside-out.

Turpin found himself compelled to trail at Clarke's heels, not a rôle he relished. He was used to being the focus of attention where anything connected with Energetics General was concerned. Now and then he tried to involve himself in one of Clarke's conversations.

'Think that print will give you a lead to — ?'

'Hell, no. Second commonest brand on the market, fourth commonest size.' And back to a technical discussion with the forensic experts.

'Whoever did it came down the track, as I see it, and then — '

'Doesn't follow.' With even greater curtness. 'We shan't know until we've finished searching the beach.'

So Turpin, anxious, withdrew into the background and smoked a rapid succession of cigarettes, his earlier confidence oozing away under the simultaneous pressure of Clarke's snubbing and the glare from the sunlight on the sand, which threatened to give him a headache. He was on the point of confronting Clarke directly and saying that he was going home because he was tired of wasting time, when the men working over the beach discovered something that made his heart lurch.

In a direct line between the dirt road and the sea, a probing metal rod had come back from six inches underground smeared with some sort of sticky plastic goo.

Oh, my God. Sheklov's survival suit!

None of his reaction showed in his face, of course, or his manner. He had had far too long to practise concealment of his emotions. Moreover, he had been assured that the destruct process left no single compound in the mess which could be identified as of foreign origin.

But suppose they underestimated the impact of thirty years' paranoia on our forensic techniques?

He wondered briefly what 'they' and 'our' meant to him nowadays.

Now it was definite. He would not dare to leave here before he had planted in Clarke's mind the seed of the suspicion Sheklov had proposed: the idea that some rival corporation, or the Navy, had decided to undermine confidence in EG's ability to fulfil its defence contracts.

Waiting for his chance, he stood by while the forensic team, with the patience of archaeologists, uncovered the mass of mingled plastic and sand. It bore no resemblance to the form of a human being, Turpin realised with relief. It had been folded roughly square, and the destruct process had caused streels of plastic to flow away from its edge like pseudopods around a sick amoeba. He waited tensely for Clarke's opinion of the find.

'What do you think?' the security man said finally to the nearest of his aides.

The man shrugged. 'Garbage,' he answered. 'One of those self-destruct bags you have on yachts, chucked overboard and washed up here.'

'That's what it looks like to me,' Clarke agreed. 'But take a sample to the lab just in case. And keep on looking. Say — uh — Turpin! I'd like a word with you now.'

He gestured for the older man to fall in at his side, and led the way towards the vegetation fringing the shore. As he walked he produced and offered a pack of cigars, a good West Coast brand.

Accepting one, Turpin decided to risk a bit of deduction himself. He said, 'Did you get hauled back from a vacation?'

'Not exactly,' Clarke grunted. 'Just my first free week-end in two months. I was out in Oregon last week, and I have cousins in Frisco, so I thought I'd take the chance to call on them. Then this blows up, so fast I don't even have the time to change clothes! Hah!' He bit the end off his cigar and spat it savagely into a nearby bush.

Well, that would excuse some of his bad manners. . . Offering a light, Turpin ventured, 'Have you drawn any conclusions yet? Naturally, on behalf of EG, I'm very concerned about all this.'

'Whereas I have to be concerned about it on behalf of the whole nation,' Clarke said, with the air of a man scoring a debating-point.

'Naturally!' Turpin agreed, lighting his own cigar. 'But, you see — '

'Just a moment.' Clarke pushed his cigar to the corner of his mouth, where it jutted up at the traditional tycoon's angle, and reached into one of the pockets of his windbreaker. He drew out something of shiny metal, about six inches long when unfolded, touched a switch at its base, and — holding it about the height of his mouth — turned through a complete circle. A high-pitched hum made Turpin's teeth ache slightly.

'Parabolic mike detector?' he said after a pause.

'Yes. And it's okay. No one is eavesdropping right now.' Clarke folded the gadget and put it away. 'Sorry, but I had to make absolutely certain, because of what I want to ask you. Turpin, how well do you know these service crews of EG's?'

'I know some of them in fair detail,' Turpin said, wondering if he was about to receive a gift from the gods. It certainly sounded as though he was. 'As to this one, thirty-three — well, rather less than some.'

'I noticed you call the crew-boss by his first name,' Clarke probed.

112

'Oh, that's company policy,' Turpin said with an easy smile. 'Executives call crew-bosses by their first names, their juniors by their surnames. It goes for both sexes.'

'I see. But it's rather an *unusual* name, isn't it — Gunnar?'

Ah!

Smoothly, never saying anything outright which might be interpreted as an accusation, Turpin laid down parameters for Clarke's thinking: someone who felt handicapped by a foreign name, possibly suspecting that he'd been passed over for promotion because of it, might so easily have listened to blandishments from another company, hoping to augment the income he regarded as less than his just due. . . He managed to refer to EG's excellent record on industrial espionage, then to the intense competition against which the firm had secured the automatic defences contract, then to the clean bill which every House committee had given them after an investigation, and all the time Clarke listened intently, now and then making a further check with his detector.

At last he gave a thoughtful nod. He said, 'I guess you must have studied Sandstrom's file.'

'Seen it, certainly,' Turpin said, blinking. 'Can't swear to having memorised it, naturally.'

'I seem to recall, though' — with a frown — 'he gave one special reason for moving into high-grade electronics, didn't he?'

'Ah. . . ' Simultaneous, a search of memory and preparation of an adequate excuse for not remembering. Memory dealt him a trump just in time. 'Why, yes! I do know what you mean. Didn't it have something to do with a childhood fascination with the space programme?'

'So he deposed,' Clarke agreed, slipping his detector back in his pocket for the fourth or fifth time. And then, just as Turpin was preparing to congratulate him on being able to pick that single entry out of heaven knew how many security files — which, indeed, was a rather sobering feat and indicated just why Clarke was as high as he was in the hierarchy of his force — he did something which took Turpin absolutely by surprise. He bent to the ground, caught up a small rock, and hurled it as far as he could.

'Did you see *that* go into orbit?' he demanded savagely. And added, before Turpin could frame words to reply with: 'Come on — better get back and see if my men have turned up anything else.'

18

'I guess that's the place,' Lora said doubtfully, slowing the car alongside a vacant parking-bay and pointing across the street to an ugly old building with a hoverhalt on its roof.

'Yes,' she added, craning to read a sign pointing to it. 'I remember the name. Right first time — not bad, hm?'

She backed into the bay and jumped out. Copying her, Sheklov stared at the building. It was shabby, with great cracks in its walls which were only prevented from spreading by the reinforced concrete beams doing double duty as supports for the steel stairs up to the hoverhalt. They had arrived at the same moment as a hovercar, and he could see the walls trembling under the extra load.

He shook his head. He hoped he wasn't going to have to spend long in this paradoxical country: so rich, yet with so many people in it prepared to suffer intolerable indignities!

Having stuffed five bucks into the nearby meter — the regular fee for two hours' parking on a Sunday — Lora caught his arm and hurried him across the street. On the steep stairs of the hoverhalt he lost sight of her as the hovercar discharged a crowd of people numbering only about twenty but blocking the width of the steps as efficiently as a small army, then caught up with her again on the landing outside the topmost apartment, where she was already ringing the bell.

Shortly, the door was opened to a security stop by a woman with a strong face and coarse black hair, who could have been any age from thirty to fifty, wearing a casual red sweater and tan pants. Her expression, resigned at first, changed in a moment to one of welcome.

'Oh! I wasn't expecting anyone, so I thought it might be the pigs — or one of my clients turning up without an appointment. But you're Lora Turpin, aren't you? Come on in!'

She released the security stop and flung the door wide.

Lora hesitated, while Sheklov's eyes seized greedily on what details of the interior of the apartment he could make out from where he stood. Books — twenty times as many as in the whole of the Turpins' home. A ouija board, hung from the wall on a bit of string. Visible on a low table, abandoned presumably when the bell rang, a tarot pack.

It was like coming home.

So who was this woman, anyway — Danty's mistress? That seemed unlikely. Vaguely he heard Lora asking whether Danty was in; equally vaguely, he registered the reply: 'No, but he could be back at any time. Please come in and wait if you'd like to.'

'Well. . . ' Lora looked to Sheklov for guidance.

'That's very kind,' he exclaimed, and this time took her arm, encouraging her over the threshold. 'Apparently you know Lora,' he added. 'I'm Don Holtzer.'

'Oh, yes. Danty said he met you at the Turpins'. I'm Magda Hansen.' Shutting the door and waving them to chairs. 'Do sit down. Maybe you'd like some coffee?'

'Please,' Sheklov said firmly.

'I'll go plug the percolator in. Just a moment.' And she headed for the miniature kitchen in the corner.

Out of the side of her mouth, looking ill-at-ease, Lora whispered, 'But that's the — uh — the girl Danty's living with. I saw her when I woke up this morning. That was why I. . . '

'Turned tail?' Sheklov supplied equally softly, finally putting two and two together. 'Well, she doesn't seem to mind your coming to call, does she?'

116

And that was all he had the chance to say before she was back and sitting down on one of the built-in couches, facing them. Recollecting her tarot cards, she leaned forward to gather them up. Sheklov decided to risk commenting on them.

'That's an unusual deck you have there? Is it what they call — uh — tarrot?' Mispronouncing it deliberately.

'Yes.' Collapsing the cards with strong thick fingers into a neat pile. 'Haven't you seen them before? Like to look?'

'Well, thanks,' Sheklov said, reaching to the full stretch of his arm to take them from her. He realised at once they were a design he didn't know. But good. The hanged man, in particular: a negro surrounded by hooded Klansmen. Very apt. He gave them back, and Magda turned to park them on a vacant section of one of the many bookshelves at her back.

'Did you say you thought it might be police at the door?' he inquired, since Lora appeared to be tongue-tied.

'Could have been,' Magda said with a sigh. 'Those radiated pigs are on a harassment kick right now — come crashing in, mostly on Sundays or in the middle of the night — just to turn everything over and make a mess. If they break a few things, so much the better.'

'But — uh — what excuse do they have for. . .?' Sheklov let the question trail away, thinking of the days when that had been the perennial nightmare of anyone on the other side who had dared to reveal an original turn of mind.

Magda gave a shrug. 'Oh, they always say "suspicion of illegal drugs", you know. But that's so much shit. It's just the thing they don't need a warrant for. Fact is, they hate rebs, and that's all there is to it.'

'I see,' Sheklov said, for want of any better comment. He felt at a loss. This woman, much older than Danty, had a similar disconcerting quality in her dark gaze and

in her tone of voice. He could almost imagine himself saying something to her, as he had done to Danty, which
would be a betrayal of his cover, and without being able
to help it even though he realised it was happening.

Still, he had to put some questions about Danty because of what had already happened. He said, 'Ah. . . Well,
if it's Danty they're after, I can't see why. I talked to him
a bit at the party last night, and he seemed to be very —
uh — serious. Sort of thoughtful. And well-read, too,' he
added as an afterthought.

'Yes,' Lora chimed in. 'That's why Don wanted to see
him again. Wasn't it, Don?'

'Yes. Yes, of course.'

There was a dead silence, during which Magda looked
— not discourteously, just searchingly — at both of them
in turn for long seconds. She said at last, 'And, of course,
the pigs don't like foster-rebs, either.'

Meaning herself, Sheklov deduced. The term had been
included in his briefings. It applied to an older person who
actively encouraged the young to drop out of society in
search of some allegedly superior truth. A few states had
incorporated it into their criminal codes, making such
encouragement an offence for which the parents of minors
could sue, by analogy with 'alienation of affection' in
the old British common law.

*Shades of Socrates and the hemlock! 'Corrupting our
Youth'!*

'I get the impression,' Sheklov said slowly, not looking
directly at Magda, 'that over the border we — you know
I'm Canadian?'

'Danty did mention it.'

Was there mockery in those dark eyes? Had she seen
through his pretence? He couldn't tell. He ploughed
doggedly on.

'Well, we seem to understand something different by
the word reb. I mean, it's not something the police would
— uh. . .' A wave of his hand.

'Down here the police pounce on anyone who's in the slightest degree different,' Magda said. 'Anyone who tries to think for himself, to begin with — they're the most dangerous of all. Every loyal citizen is convinced that the government is right, even if today it says the exact opposite of what it said yesterday. Not that that happens so much any more. We've decayed into what they call a consensus.' She made the word sound faintly obscene.

'You mean — ' Lora began. Magda cut her short.

'What I mean is that the government of this country is killing us. Stone-dead. By slow strangulation.'

She jolted forward on her couch, her face suddenly animated, and Sheklov realised with a start that she was beautiful — not in the conventional American, or even the conventional Russian, sense, which had more to do with mere glamour, but in the ancient sense of the Gioconda or the Venus di Milo. It was as though a light had been switched on inside her head which illuminated her true personality. Also, in contrast with the shrill whine of almost every other woman he had met since his arrival — most notably, Sophie Turpin and her mother — her voice was a resonant contralto, cello-forceful.

'And it's a tough job for them,' she said. 'Because in every generation you get a handful of people who won't just be crushed into the regulation mould. Don't you? The ones who want to be — oh — inventors, rather than engineers, or poets rather than copywriters, or architects rather than building-contractors. Peg it?'

'I guess so,' Sheklov said, and added wryly, 'Likewise, ecologists rather than timber-salesmen.'

'You peg,' she said, and this time smiled at him — just with her eyes, wrinkling the lids humorously. 'So what happens when you block off all their opportunities to explore and experiment as they want to? You get rebs. Hell, you're bound to.'

'Well — sure you are!' Sheklov said, blinking. 'So. . .?'

'So they get stamped on,' Magda said. 'Like I said.'

'But — '

'But why? Oh, I know it's crazy. I know we're so rich we ooze money like — like fat dripping off roast pork. I know we ought to be able to tolerate a fraction of one per cent of young people who'd rather sit and think than fit into the machine. But people seem to resent their need to do that, don't they?'

Sheklov swallowed hard, wondering what Holtzer ought to say, and was saved the trouble. Lora spoke up.

'I know just what you mean!' she exclaimed. 'Lots of times I think inside my head there's something going on which isn't in the books they make you read in school. It makes me want to do crazy things now and then, really *crazy*, just to shake everybody up. And they don't even *notice!*' The last word was almost a cry.

'So what do you do about it?' Magda said.

'I. . .' She licked her lips. Eventually she shook her head and stared down at her hands, folded in her lap.

'See, Don?' Magda said. 'That's what a foster-reb like me is trying to stop. Someone like Lora ought to be able to — to *go* somewhere, *do* something, stack up new experience and dig around among it in case the answer's somewhere underneath.'

'I — uh — I guess I can see you have a case there,' Sheklov said cautiously. 'But what one hears about the result. . .'

'You mean the popular picture of a reb?' Magda interrupted. 'I guess if you're Canadian' (did she lay too much stress on that or was his imagination working overtime?) 'you've been fooled by the media. I'm not talking about fakes, phoneys, borderline psychopaths, what they used to wrap up under one handy label like 'beat' or 'hippie'. That went out of style when the courts started holding that long hair was *prima-facie* proof of vagrancy because it meant you couldn't pay the barber, and the pigs grunted with joy and reached for their guns!'

Reflexively Sheklov touched his chin. Back There he'd

sported a beard. Why not, in an area where the winter temperatures regularly dipped to −30° Centigrade.

'Yeah, beards too,' Magda agreed. 'And when that happened the phoneys folded up and went home. Leaving just the few, just the handful, who couldn't be folded up. And what can they do? If they apply for a passport, the pigs come running and turn over their homes, grill their families, their friends, until no one wants to know them any more. "Everything's great here, why should you want to leave?" — that's the principle, and saying you're curious about the rest of the world is no excuse. You've been told all your life that this country is the best, the finest, the most wonderful. So they want to know why you aren't satisfied. And how can you say why you aren't? You haven't done the things that might tell you!'

'But if you do try and leave, you have to leave for good!' Lora burst out. 'I've thought about it, and — and I just daren't! I might get shot at the border!'

'A lot of people do,' Magda sighed. 'Which is why most rebs go exploring in a different direction altogether.'

Sheklov looked at the ouija board, the tarot deck, various other significant items on display. He said at last, 'You must mean — inside their heads.'

'Yes.' Magda gave him a puzzled look. 'I usually have to spell that out to people when I'm defending the rebs. I guess north of the border you aren't quite so calcified, hm? But that's the long and short of it, yes.'

'How did you get involved with these rebs?' Sheklov queried. 'If you don't mind my asking.'

Magda seemed to be overcome with a fit of self-consciousness. She said, avoiding his eyes, 'Oh! Oh, I guess I was one of the half-and-half cases. Sometimes I felt I ought to stand up for what I believed in, and sometimes I was just lazy enough to coast along with the gang, and I drifted into a marriage on that basis. Which turned sour, and taught me — much too late — that my laziness was a crime against myself. And, too, I found out that I

121

have. . .'

'Yes?' Sheklov prompted.

'I have a talent,' Magda said after a brief hesitation, and pointed at the card in the window. It was so thin the word CONSULTATIONS could be read on it, backwards, against the light sky of late afternoon. 'You see,' she continued, licking her lips, 'I do have more — uh — empathy than some people. I trained as a nurse when I quit college, thinking maybe I'd go to work for the Red Cross or some other international aid organisation, in some broken-backed poverty-stricken country. It turned out I wasn't allowed to, because — well, because I'd been kind of wild as a kid and they wouldn't give a passport to anyone with a drug-bust on their record. Smoking pot was all, but quite enough. So here I am, a professional shoulder to weep on in an age when most people won't admit they can cry. Won't even confide in their best friends. It doesn't require a licence, so that's cool.'

Sheklov was framing his next question, when Lora spoke up again unexpectedly. She said, 'Say — uh — Magda. Does Danty have any kind of talent? I kind of wondered when. . . Did he tell you how we met? He saved my life!'

Sheklov rounded on her in astonishment. There was something so brittle and superficial about this girl, hearing her utter a statement like that jolted him.

But Magda was nodding as though it was perfectly natural to say such things. 'Oh, that Danty!' she said, in a tone which cross-bred cynicism with affection. 'He has a talent, sure has. Know what he always says about himself?'

Lora shook her head, her eyes hungry.

'Ever read *The Sword in the Stone?* Yes? Remember Merlin the magician?'

'Yes, of course!'

'Well, Danty always says he's in the same mess, born at the wrong end of time. You see, he — '

There came a scratching at the door, the sound of a key being fumbled into the lock. She broke off and swung around to face that way. So did the others. The door flew wide.

Danty stood there, swaying drunkenly, lips drawn back in a grimace of pain, eyes almost closed, a crusting cut on his forehead, and a great blood-gushing slash on his left arm which now, letting fall his key, he struggled again to staunch with his red right hand.

'Help me,' he whispered faintly, and fell headlong.

19

Lora screamed.

Galvanised by the sound, Sheklov leapt from his chair. He slapped the door shut at the full reach of his arm and dropped to his knees beside Danty.

'Shut up!' he rasped at Lora. 'Go find a phone, call a doctor! Magda, help me get him on the couch! We'll need ice — scissors — bandages — '.

Coolly she undercut him, bending over his shoulder to inspect Danty's wound. 'I did train as a nurse, remember?' she murmured. And put one hand accurately on a pressure-point which reduced the surging leakage of blood to an ooze.

'Oh. Yes, of course. Sorry.' Sheklov rose.

'And you?' she pursued. 'Are you trained in medicine too?'

What have I said now? Sheklov's mind raced. But almost at once he hit on a good reason for Holtzer to know first-aid.

'Hell, of course! Do you have any idea how many lumbermen lose arms and legs to power-saws every year? Must be hundreds!'

'Good, then,' Magda said. 'Lora, bring ice-cubes, will you? And you'll find a box in the corner of the kitchen — top shelf — marked with a red cross. I'll need that.'

'What about calling a doctor?' Sheklov snapped. 'Don't you have a phone?'

Magda gave him a steady look. 'Think I can afford indemnity insurance?'

'What?'

124

'It's very clear you're not American! You want a doctor who makes house-calls, you have to pay insurance against his being mugged or robbed on the way to you. In Cowville the going rate's a thousand a month.' She added after a moment, 'Anyway, Danty's black, and no white doctor would treat him, and I wouldn't dare call a black one. Help me lift him to that couch — no, just a moment, I'll put a sheet on it.'

He left a bloody trail on the floor.

After that Sheklov reacted mechanically as Magda efficiently cut away Danty's sleeve, wiped the knife wound — that was what it had to be, an inch wide and more than that deep — and sprayed it in turn with an analgesic, an antibiotic powder, and finally with a clear solution from an aerosol can. Reading the label on this last before Lora dutifully returned it to the first-aid kit, Sheklov learned that it was intended to create a film impervious to airborne infection which would contract as it dried and draw the edges of a cut together, obviating the need to insert stitches.

Hmm! That would be useful at home! A fine invention!
On the other hand, he wouldn't care to live in a society which found it necessary to include such a product in a home first-aid kit. . .

Then the final touches: rinsing of Danty's face — his forehead cut was minor, hardly more than a scratch, although his eyes would be puffy for a day or two, Magda predicted — and the job of clearing up, which Lora undertook silently, despite her faintly green cheeks and look of incipient nausea. Magda complimented her a couple of times on being so helpful, and she flashed smiles of gratitude in response.

Sheklov recalled what she had said about her parents not taking an interest in their children.

At some point during all this — Sheklov did not notice exactly when — Danty regained consciousness, but ap-

125

parently figured out what was going on and went on lying quite still. His first word, when Magda had done with him, was, 'Thanks.'

'You're all right, Danty?' Lora exploded, and almost let the bowl of pink water she was carrying to the kitchen fall to the floor. Barely in time she recovered, parked it on the table, and fell on her knees at his side.

'Me? Sure, baby, I'm okay. I'm tough,' Danty said, ruffling her hair. 'Let me sit up, hm? That's the idea' — as she twisted around to support him behind his shoulders. Touching his arm, he winced, and added, 'I guess this may need a sling for a day or two, Magda.'

'Lora, go look behind that curtain, by my bed. There's a bagful of rags,' Magda said, and Lora departed at a run. She added to Danty, 'Who did it — Josh?'

'I'm not sure whether Josh beat Shark to it, or the other way around,' Danty sighed. 'They took me completely by surprise. Jumped me near the hoverhalt as I was coming off the beach.'

'You know who did this to you?' Sheklov said, astonished. 'Shouldn't you — uh — report it, then? Or something?' he added lamely.

'To the pigs?' Danty said with a cynical grin. 'Man, I should die laughing the day the pigs do anything for me! More like they'd give Josh a medal.'

'Is this long enough?' Lora called, waving a piece of blue cloth around the corner of the curtain which hid Magda's sleeping-alcove. Magda held out her hand for it, and after tugging hard on its ends folded and tied it to make a sling.

'Great, baby,' Danty said, having tried it out. 'Say, I guess I should thank you all, shouldn't I? Don — Lora. . . Lora, honey! Shit, what you crying for?'

She was struggling not to, but tears were pouring down her cheeks and she was clamping her hands together to stop them shaking.

'Give her a trank!' Danty said, and interrupted himself.

'No, got a better idea. Any of that vodka left that Punchy gave us?'

'Sure is,' Magda said, snapping her fingers, and headed for the kitchen. She was back in a moment with mismatched glasses and a bottle half-full. According to its label, Sheklov noted, the contents were made in Schenectady, New York. This wasn't like the Vyborova he drank at home, but it helped, and he set his empty glass aside gratefully. It was only when he found Danty offering the bottle for a refill that he realised he had drunk it Russian-style, in a gulp, instead of sipping it like the rest of them.

That, though, apparently wasn't unexpected in the present context. At least, none of them commented.

After a pause to wipe her eyes, Lora said suddenly, 'I — uh — I'd like to say something.'

'So shoot,' invited Danty.

'I. . .' She took the plunge. 'I like you. Both of you! You feel *real*.'

'That's a change from this morning,' Danty chuckled. 'I thought you'd set the stairs afire, the speed you left at.'

'I know,' Lora said, almost inaudibly. 'All the time I do stupid things, the exact opposite of what I want. . . I wish *I* could figure out how to explore inside myself, too. I'm sure there's something in there I ought to know about, something that would be worth having. After all, I'm not an idiot. I'm just' — a furious grimace — 'kind of crazy!'

'Aren't we all?' Magda said, and drained her glass. At the same moment there was a shrill ring from behind the curtain, and she jumped up.

'That might be about Molly,' she said, answering an unspoken query from Danty. 'I left the number at the hospital so they could tell us the news.' And vanished.

'Friend of ours,' Danty explained. 'Pregnant.'

'Oh. Is she in the maternity ward?' Sheklov hazarded.

127

He gave his usual crooked grin. 'No. Emergency. They have three kids already and their neighbours aren't talking to them. So her husband threw her downstairs to try and abort her. Broke her pelvis.'

'What?' Lora burst out in horror.

'Happens all the time,' Danty said, passing his unhurt hand wearily over his face. 'Shit, what you expect? We got three hundred sixty million people now, and no way out.'

There was silence among them. During it, they heard Magda's voice.

'But how the hell did you get this number? It's unlisted, and I never gave it to Avice!'

'Oh,' Danty said softly. 'Not Molly. One of her patients — I mean clients. Mustn't say "patient". You have to have a licence if you have patients.'

Magda again: 'Yes. Yes, all right! Thanks for calling. But don't use this number again, and above all don't pass it on to anyone else, is that clear? I don't want to have it changed again!'

And she came back, scowling.

'The Clarke woman?' Danty asked.

'Right in one.' She helped herself to more vodka and resumed her seat. 'Husband's been called back unexpectedly, so she won't dare come here tomorrow. Christ, can you call that sort of thing a marriage? That's what mine was like, you know, why it broke up. I wasn't allowed to do anything I thought of by myself, or I'd get kicked in the ass for my temerity.' She threw her liquor down her throat as though it would drown the memory.

'Danty!' Lora said suddenly, jumping out of her chair and going to sit at his side. 'Are you okay now? Feeling all right?'

'No,' Danty said. 'I'm feeling lousy — what the hell do you expect, with a crack on the head and a knife-cut?' And relented, reaching up to tousle her hair affectionately. 'Don't let it get you down, though. I've had worse

things happen to me, and lived through them. . . Say,
Mag'!'

'Yes?'

'Could we like feed these people? Day's wearing on,
and all I had was brunch.'

'Well — '

'Hold it!' Sheklov interrupted. 'I have a better idea.
Why don't we all eat dinner together? My expense. Lora,
would you drive us somewhere? Like maybe out of town?'

'Oh, great!' Lora said. 'Sure, wonderful! Danty?'

'Well, I wouldn't say no, if we can find somewhere that
doesn't mind a mixed party,' Danty said after a pause.
'What about you, Mag'?'

'I guess so,' she said. 'Have to change clothes first,
though, if we're going any place — uh — respectable.'

'So will I,' Danty said, getting up. 'But I sure wouldn't
refuse a square meal. Thanks, Don. We won't be a moment.'

He caught Magda by the arm and escorted her through
the curtain, out of sight.

The moment they were alone in the sleeping alcove, she
rounded on him. Very softly, but very ferociously, because this must not carry to the others, she said, 'What
the *shit* possessed you to walk into that much trouble?'
She tapped his cut arm.

'Had to,' was the curt reply. 'Just *had* to. Know what
happened this afternoon? Turpin was called out from
home to go somewhere very fast in an EG veetol. And I
can guess where.'

'That reserved area?' Magda said, her eyes fixed on his
drawn face.

'Where else? And for some reason it was more important for me to know that than for me to steer clear of
where Josh and Shark and Potatohead might find me.'

There was an awful dead pause.

'Remember what I said about getting scared?' Danty

said at last. 'What — what — *what* could be more important than my keeping alive? And I mean that! They were going to cut me into little pieces, and no one would have tried to help! It was just luck that there was a pig somewhere around who wasn't fond of them right now. I got the notion that Shark and Potatohead were like having a blow on the beach, and the pig moved them on. So when he saw them again. . . ' A vague gesture. 'That was all that saved me. I rode the hoverline back here, bleeding all over the car, and you know nobody even offered me a seat?'

'That's America,' Magda said.

'Yes.' Danty turned away and pulled open the small built-in closet where his clothes were stored. 'And you know something? *I want out.*'

'Where to? Africa? Look what happened to the people who went there in the Black Exodus!'

'No, just *out,*' Danty said. His voice, still barely above a whisper, suddenly became level and determined. 'Any place where this fucking talent would have something solid to work on, instead of walking me into trouble all the time!'

20

'That you, Morton?' Fenella Clarke called as she heard
the key clicking in the door. A microphone beside her
chair picked up her voice — being directionalised, it did
not blur the question by also picking up the sound from
the TV she was watching — and conveyed it to the
entrance foyer.

'Who the hell else are you expecting who can get
through these locks?' her husband retorted. There was a
mike focused on him, too.

When she married him, she had thought it romantic, in
some indefinable way, to have captured one of the
brightest up-and-coming young experts who had undertaken that toughest of all varieties of law-enforcement
work: policing the very minds of disloyal citizens. And
her confidence had been amply repaid in material terms.
Less than five years after their meeting, he had been in a
position to buy into the Lakonia towers, and this apartment was among the choicest, with a superb view on
every side.

The kind of thing she had not foreseen. . .

Well, that mike beside her chair was an example.
(Remembering, she said to it meekly, 'Just a figure of
speech, honey, you know that!' And heard a grunt by
way of response.) The whole place was riddled, perme-
ated, *infested* with bugs. Electronic type. Mostly newly-
developed gadgetry which he was field-testing, because his
profession was also his hobby.

And, above all, she had never in her life imagined the
penalties she was going to have to pay for her comfort. In

her memory, she marked the turning-point by Morton's decision to have a separate bedroom in their Lakonia apartment — not by the acquisition of the apartment itself. It was at that stage that he had reached the point where a Security Force executive began to worry about talking in his sleep. At least, that was what she had worked out in discussions with her friend Avice Donnelly, who was married to a senior plant security officer for Energetics General and hence was regarded as a proper person for Morton Clarke's wife to befriend.

She didn't actually *like* Avice. She found her bitchy, over-fond of gossip and especially of scandal, and given to nursing ridiculous grudges, sometimes for years on end. But one couldn't get along with no friends whatever. Just couldn't! No matter how often Morton indicated that that was the way he would have preferred it.

Every promotion seemed to make things worse. Back when he was a mere agent, and they had been courting, he had appeared to get some kind of *fun* out of his work. That was something she could understand, even appreciate. There was a quality akin to fencing in the person-to-person duels of a subversive and a security agent, and when the results were in, one could stand back and look at the ingenuity that had led to the dénouement with honest admiration. 'He thought that we would think. . . ' Only: 'We realised he would think that we would think. . . '

And he'd been promoted to the next grade, keeper, and she'd accepted his proposal of marriage on the spot. He'd been so overjoyed, it was infectious!

The rot set in later. She found out about his promotion to acting bailiff by chance, weeks after it was authorised. . . then to substantive bailiff only when she answered a call on the secure line while they were discussing the household accounts. . .

She had barely dared to mention all this to anyone except Avice, because if Morton felt he had to keep such data from his wife, how could she talk about it with any-one else?

And, naturally, there was the problem of children. Fenella had hoped to have at least one — people felt that was okay — and had looked forward to the baby's arrival. Except Morton refused to co-operate. A child was vulnerable to being kidnapped by subversives.

She had asked about divorce when that episode over-took her. And been refused. Flatly. *No.*

And tomorrow, like Avice, she had meant to pour out her heart to this wonderful woman, this Magda Hansen, who was so sympathetic and understanding and made such fabulous suggestions for getting around obstinate husbands, and. . .

How the hell had Avice brought herself to consult Mrs Hansen, anyway? Avice with her impenetrable shell of self-possession, her tinkly laugh, her air of not giving a fart about anyone or anything — she must have been driven to breaking-point.

Come to think of it, I haven't heard from her in over three weeks! I should have called up. . .

She reached for a cigarette, the latest of far too many today, and glanced towards the door. Wasn't Morton going to come in?

Obviously not. But then, he so often didn't. Just made straight for his den, which she was forbidden to enter un-less he was present.

One of these days I'm going to walk in there and smear shit all over all the things he prizes more than me. And then I'll shoot myself right in the middle of it, the mess-iest way possible, through the roof of my mouth. See how he likes coming home and finding that lot to clear up!

She turned her attention, with an effort, back to the TV, knowing at the bottom of her mind that she never would.

133

Stomach grumbling from the sandwich and glass of milk
he had gulped down on his way home, at the wrong time
owing to his hasty departure from California — at least as
far as his metabolism was concerned — Morton Clarke
wiped his face as he entered his den and closed the door.
Tight. With a careful double-check of the locks.

*Should have remained a bachelor. No life for a married
man, my career.*

But, having married, one must stay married. They were
instantly suspicious, in the Security Force, of anyone who
changed his mind on such an important matter. . .

He sat down before his desk, which was more of an
electronic console because this was his only permissible
outlet for personal initiative once he had dedicated his
life to the security of his country. Sometimes he thought
of himself as akin to a medieval monk, sustained only by
recollection of a pledge he had given while in full and
sober possession of his faculties when the Rule of his
order became intolerable. Yes; he must not give way to
private preferences, to personal predilections. This afternoon, at the reserved area, he had come perilously close
to doing so when he picked up that rock and uttered
that fierce remark to Turpin: 'Did you see it go into
orbit?'

What went into orbit, these days, from the United
States, was the minimum necessary to preserve the nation
from the unceasing hostility of the rest of the world. That
had been drilled into him ever since, back in college, he
had first become aware of the burgeoning commitment
within his mind, and realised he was going to find fulfil-
ment only in working for the safety and salvation of his
native land.

He raised his eyes to the one item he permitted to
decorate his sanctum. It wasn't — as one might have
expected — Old Glory, or even a photo of Prexy. He knew
too much about the workings of modern American
government to have chosen anything of that sort. No: he

had fixed to the wall where he could see it any time he looked up something which reminded him of the penalties you had to pay for freedom: a newspaper cutting, glassed and framed, from the Chinese official paper *Red Banner*, and it showed a North Vietnamese official press photo of a captured American pilot being led on a rope halter through the streets of Hanoi. He couldn't read the caption, but a friend of his had translated it for him, and a typed summary had been pasted under the actual cutting. It said that because this man had committed the crime of bombing Angkor Wat he was plainly a hopeless case for re-education — quote/unquote — and hence had been condemned to public ignominy.

Shit! What good are a bunch of ancient ruins when men's minds are in chains?

Sight of that picture, as always, re-stimulated him to the ever-greater urgency of his task. He drew a deep breath and started to punch the various keyboards set into his desk. First off: anti-bug checks.

All clear. No one had located any of the lines with any tapping device known to Security Force experts. He was as safe from eavesdropping here as at the SF headquarters.

Thank heaven. . .

Next, therefore: a summary of things which had occurred to him since leaving the reserved area. The forensic team, naturally, would be there indefinitely, but another top SF executive had arrived half an hour ago and relieved him, and he had been permitted to depart. On the way back to Lakonia, though, his mind had whirled and whirled, like a turbine under power, and now he had to report his thoughts.

He recited, tonelessly, for about ten minutes into the proper phone, summing up all his views concerning that notion of Turpin's — that the site might have been inactivated by an agent of some rival corporation caring more about profits than national security, or perhaps by

Navy, who had of course had their noses out of joint for more than a decade. It was entirely too possible that Turpin was right; at least, nothing on his record, or that of any other EG board-member, indicated that there would be likelier suspects within the corporation.

However, he dutifully listed the various doubts he was entertaining.

That done, he switched his attention to other matters. What additional data might be relevant? To punch for records of shoe-sales that might have included the agent of that footprint, so sharp and clear on the roadway leading into the site — no, that was absurd. They sold millions of pairs of shoes every month, and, as he'd told Turpin the brand-name was one of the commonest. (*Shit! A 'clue' in classic form, and here I am helpless, staring at it in my memory!*)

On the other hand, if someone had come to and gone away from the site on the morning in question. . . He put his chin in his hand and stared at nothing. Well, there was so much traffic on the superways nowadays, a thorough sifting of every vehicle that passed within a few miles of any of the three thousand reserved areas would take even computers a very long time. . . and that was assuming there were records to analyse.

Suppose, though, a patrolman had filed some sort of trivial report during the period immediately following the shut-down of the site? The auto-logs had stopped registering at about oh-three-fifty; dawn had been — uh — between four and five. . .

He reached for the remote keyboard that connected him with the master forensic computer at his HQ, and punched into it an inquiry that seemed like a fair compromise: had any patrolman in the vicinity reported anything, no matter how minor, during the appropriate period, which didn't appear in any of the regular traffic-offence categories? He wasn't certain quite what he was looking for, but — well, surely a saboteur must have come to the site, spent a short while in and around it, and then gone away. Something as simple as a car reported travelling in one direction, then in the opposite direction sooner than could be accounted for by a stopover and turnaround at a nearby city: that would fit.

Sifting police records was inevitably slow, even for computers; so many matters nowadays were police business. Waiting, he decided he could legitimately take care of a personal problem which had been irking him since his return home. What about Fenella? What had she been up to?

Should have remained a bachelor. . .

But he hadn't and since he had a wife, she must be like Caesar's, above reproach. It was not strictly permissible to adapt officially-issued detection gear for purposes like suspected infidelity, but of course all the married executives in the Security Force did so, and the top brass turned a blind eye. He himself had Fenella so thoroughly bugged, she literally couldn't go to the bathroom — let alone make a phone-call or take a cab-ride — without his being able to find out afterwards.

It took him less than three minutes to locate, on the tapes, the argument she had had with the phone company to try and get them to release the unlisted number of Magda Hansen.

21

'There are two ways you can go,' Magda said suddenly, after a long period of near-silence during which the night-black ribbon of the superway had unreeled like a tape punctuated with blasts of random noise, the glare of on-coming lights at the curves where suddenly they shone direct — for a mere fraction of a second — on to Shek-lov's tortured retinae.

'What?' He glanced at her in surprise, thinking she must be giving him advice for their route back to Cowville. But there was no intersection sign ahead, and the last in-structions he had read from the roadside had informed him it was twenty-three miles to the next exit.

'Two ways you can go,' Magda repeated. 'Into your-self — or out of the world that other people share. Apart from that, you can't go anywhere and still be a person.'

Sheklov pondered that. He was driving, and terribly aware that he probably was not doing it very well. He had had a ready-made excuse for that — when Lora had suggested it, and Magda had deferred, on their departure from the restaurant where they had eaten dinner and drunk a lot of wine and beer, he had produced the data incorporated in his briefing, which explained that like many Canadians he had never owned an American car, but had stuck to Swedish and Italian imports.

Still, this thing of Lora's seemed to be designed for people who didn't drive well, and certainly the roads were...

He rapidly reviewed everything which had happened or been talked about since they left Cowville on the outward leg of their trip. They had had to go a long way — north, of course — before finding a place where they would serve a mixed party with less than forced tolerance. One restaurant-owner had even offered the classic excuse: 'It's not that *I* object, mind you, only that my other customers. . . '

Goodbye!

And then it had proved to be very pleasant, although the meal was incredibly expensive and the continuous music grated on Sheklov's ears and the high voices of other diners uttering demonstrably false statements had made him now and then want to get up and beat a little common sense into their heads. Still, that wasn't his brief. He had to act as though he were what he pretended to be. Turpin's comment about being shot to death by an Army firing-squad rang continually in his brain.

So there had been no awkwardnesses until they were getting back in the car, and Lora had said outright that she intended to ride in back with Danty and not drive home. And held out the car-key for Sheklov to take.

Following which, on the dark road, occasional gasps and mutters had punctuated the music from the radio, and once, perfectly clearly, 'Danty, you're *terrific!*'

It was reaching down through Sheklov's mental armour, and hitting him in the — well, the hormones, you might say. He had entertained the notion that when they arrived back in Cowville Magda might. . .

I don't understand! I simply don't! Culture shock!

How on Earth (he consciously capitalised it) could this sort of promiscuous, casual behaviour co-exist with all the billboards he kept seeing that advertised Koenig's? That brand-name, and its implications, had been explained to him in detail; lead-impregnated, Koenig's underwear was claimed to protect the gonads from accidental irradiation, and styles were offered for women as well as men.

While the cars that whizzed past — he had proof of this at his back — were marketed with rear seats that folded down to facilitate seduction!

It dawned on him, perhaps as much as two miles later at the speed they were travelling, that Magda was offering the explanation he yearned for. . . and then he recalled that she had claimed to possess more empathy than most people, to the extent of having a talent someone in trouble could call on her to exercise.

Me too?

It made him abruptly cold to think of what she might have — not guessed, *deduced* about him. His briefing had never taken a person like her into account.

Yet he had learned to trust some of his own instinctual reactions, too, and nothing about Magda — Danty was a different matter — had made his nape prickle, his usual warning-sign. There was no hint of menace about her, just a curiosity which he found almost refreshing, as though she put the most personal possible questions without a thought of giving offence.

He said, framing his words carefully, 'I guess you must have noticed how hard this country has hit me. I mean, when I took on this job of mine, fixing that pulp-contract which brought me down here, I walked into it thinking what I guess most people think north of the border: "They're right next door, so they're probably no more different than those people down the street!" If you — uh — follow me.'

'Well, Danty and Lora aren't a hundred per cent typical,' Magda murmured, taking a cigarette from the dispenser on the dash. The EMPTY light came on as she removed it; as though by reflex, she felt for her own pack and slipped a couple into the store to compensate. The light went out. There was almost nothing on the dash that related to the operation of the car — the speedometer and the ignition-on light were almost buried among the ancillaries, the radiation-counter, the rain-detector light, the controls for the radio, and the air-conditioning instruments.

Clearly from the back: 'Oh, Dan-ty-y-y. . . !'

'You don't get it,' Magda said, having drawn and let go the first puff of her cigarette.

'Frankly, no,' Sheklov grunted, and twisted the wheel the few degrees necessary to carry them through a wide curve.

'It's like I was saying,' Magda answered with a shrug. 'When things become intolerable, the obvious way is out. In our case, you can't go out — not unless you're prepared never to come back. And Lora wasn't joking when she talked about the risk of being shot at the border. Except that treading on a mine is probably a bigger risk, and then of course the — uh — the private enterprise bit is unpredictable.'

'The what?'

'Private enterprise. Lots of privately financed organisations patrol the borders, too. And mine them. Security doesn't approve, and sometimes they get hauled into court on the grounds that if they don't trust the official patrols they can't be loyal. But usually they get let off with a nominal fine and a warning, because patriotism with a capital P is the excuse for anything.'

'I — I don't believe I ever heard about that,' Sheklov admitted, wondering when the border in his mind was going to be crossed, the one between Sheklov and Holtzer, who was fading moment by moment as he struggled with the problem that had troubled him since his arrival. . .

I'm on a fool's errand here! It's as though they'd sent me to an asylum three thousand miles wide! An idea which is brand-new could be new because it's insane, couldn't it?

Suppose I'd walked into one of the 'private enterprise' patrols when I came ashore?

Hell! Maybe I did!

'Getting tired? Like me to spell you?' Magda said. He

141

realised with a wrenching sense of panic that he had let his attention drift from the wheel, and crossed into another lane already crammed with cars.

'Uh — no,' he forced out. 'No, I'm fine.'

Providentially, in the lane just vacated, a car howled past with its governor cut out, doing far more than the legal maximum, and he was able to jerk his head at it.

'Saw him coming up — thought I'd better move over.'

'Ah — yes,' Magda said, and took another drag on her cigarette. A few heartbeats later, she continued with what she had been saying as though there had been no distraction.

'Yes! There are two ways to go, assuming you want to go somewhere and aren't just content to be forced into the official mould. You can go insane, and that's the easy one. You can buy Koenig's, and keep a gun on the dash' — there was one in this car and she tapped it with long sharp nails — 'and convince yourself you're taking the ordinary, reasonable precautions a human being has to take to protect himself. That's what I meant when I said you can go out of the world other people share.'

'But surely,' Sheklov hazarded, 'other people do share that world.'

'You miss my point. They share the idea that the world mustn't be shared. Tap a friend on the shoulder when you meet him on the street, he whirls around and pulls a gun, doesn't he? Likely a gas-gun, that only blinds and doesn't kill, but a gun nonetheless. And he fires before he looks to see whether you're known to him.'

'Yes,' Sheklov said at length, a mile of dark road later. 'I'm with you.'

'It's a whole pattern,' Magda said. 'And it's crazy. Like with warts on. You know — you ever hear — of any sane species whose worst natural enemy was himself?'

'Man?'

'*Natural* species?'

Silence except for the humming sound of traffic all

around them. Signs were beginning to say COWVILLE up ahead.

'Yes, I guess we tried to defy nature at some stage,' Sheklov said at last. 'One gets to see the results in the timber-trade, naturally — ' He caught himself as Magda gave a dry laugh and echoed his last word in a whisper: *naturally!*

'So what's the other way?' he asked, irritated.

'Hold it,' Magda said, twisting around in her seat. 'Hey! Close out, you two!'

In the back seat, a mutter of annoyance. Sheklov spared a glance in his mirror and saw the two heads, one fair and one dark, separate and move to a regular sitting position.

'What's the trouble?'

'Pigs, what else?' Magda said, and leaned away from him. A car with a spotlight on the corner of the windshield was working its way up the line of traffic, and the man next to the driver was flashing the light into the windows of the cars it passed.

When they came up to Lora's car, they found her and Danty decorously sitting, more or less fully clothed, in opposite corners of the rear seat.

'The other way?' Magda said when they had been overtaken in due sequence. 'Find a route where the bastards can't follow you and shine spotlights on you, of course.'

'There isn't one,' Lora said in a dead voice.

The turnout signs were saying COWVILLE — NORTH. Sheklov remembered that from their entry on to the superway. He slowed and signalled right.

'You're not with me,' Magda said. 'I mean the route where the things that count in your life aren't the things they're worried about — even though they ought to be afraid of them, because they're the most dangerous. Danty, are you okay?'

He was rubbing his temple with the hand of his uninjured arm.

143

'My head hurts,' he said in a dull tone.

'Oh, Danty!' Lora burst out. 'It must be that cut! Don, get us off the superway quick as you can, find a drugstore!'

'No!' Magda snapped. 'Zip it, will you? Danty?'

'I . . . ' He licked his lips. 'I don't get it all,' he said after a pause. 'But the one thing we mustn't do is go home.'

'But — !' Sheklov began.

'Make for it, sure,' Danty said. Little beads of sweat, shiny in the lights of the city, were springing out on his skin. 'But don't try and stop outside, that clear? Something's happening, something bad. We got to smell the scene and find out what.'

Sheklov gave Magda a blank stare. She sat back with a resigned expression.

'Told you,' she said. 'Danty was born at the wrong end of time, peg? So you do what he tells you. If you don't — shit, the sky may fall on us.'

22

It was a long time before Morton Clarke could believe
the impersonal report of the computers, so far away from
this familiar desk of his, yet — electronically speaking —
so close at hand that he could reach out and touch them.

They had a kind of reality to them which people never
seemed to have.

He looked again at the print-outs, dangling over the
automatic destruction unit, and eventually picked them
up and laid them side by side, because he had to convince
himself.

'The name's the same,' he said with an access of
gallows humour, and did what had to be done.

Then he waited. He didn't wonder what Fenella was
doing. He knew she was watching TV.

Channel 8.

The first thing the security forces did *nct* do was notify
the police that they were about to conduct a raid. It
wasn't safe to do that; the police were not secure, but
jealously guarded their right to pick their own men and
women, to hide their confidential files. . . or to try to.

So it had been years since the US Security Force
liaised with the police anywhere, and above all not in
Lakonia or Cowville, the most sensitive of all areas in the
country.

Cold, despite the outside warmth of the night, Clarke
sat at his desk and dictated what must be looked out for.

'Apartment empty,' was the first news that reached

him. He gave a nod. That figured.

Then, a few minutes later: 'Looks like a foster-reb pad. Mystical books. Diagrams. Ouija board, that kind of thing. Man's and woman's clothes in the closets.'

'Names?' was Clarke's only counter.

'Danty Aloysius Ward, male. Magda Hansen, née Porter. . . Say, Mr Clarke!'

'Yes?'

'What the hell are we looking for? I been in hundreds of places like this one' — a vibrating, hammering sound, the overheard passage of a hovercar — 'though maybe not all quite so noisy! Bad place to plant bugs, this!'

Maybe that's why they're there. 'Did you check the phone?'

'Sure we did. It's unlisted, but the number corresponds.'

'Ah-hah. Then tell me what size shoes they take, will you?'

'I guess it's Charlie who's checking out the clothes. I'll get him; just a moment!'

Waiting, Clarke looked again at the tape he had — well, put it politely, don't say *extracted*, say — *obtained* from the police computers.

SOURCE: LOGGED BY CLOUGH WILLIAM N., PATROLMAN #7653. LOCATION: GASTATION 132 SUPERWAY ZONE H-8. TIMED AT: —

'Mr Clarke?'

'Yes.'

'I have those shoe sizes for you. Brand-names too, where I can read them. Most of them are pretty worn.'

'Shoot, then.' Poising pen over paper.

When he had the details before him, Clarke felt his mind congealing like fresh concrete, into new hardness, new heaviness. He was barely aware of his own voice saying, 'It fits. Keep at it. Turn the apartment inside out. This one is *big.*'

After which he stared at the news-cutting framed on the wall and did nothing for nearly five minutes.

'Where's Sophie?' Mrs Gleewood demanded in the middle of a sentence uttered by the TV which she and her son-in-law were watching.

'What?' Bemused, as usual, into a semi-stupor by the polychrome images on the screen, Turpin started up in his chair. 'Oh! Sophie! Well. . . Well, I guess she went to lie down, didn't she?'

'You mean she's drunk again,' Mrs Gleewood snapped. 'I noticed at dinner — don't think you can hide that sort of thing from me! I never thought when she married you she'd be driven to alcoholism, I swear I didn't!'

She folded her bony hands and jutted her sharp chin forward. She dieted, of course, to 'keep her figure', apparently in the hope that young men would continue to find her attractive in spite of her narrow, cruel eyes with those dirty-looking dark bags under them, the chicken-skin scrawniness of her throat — which should have sported about three comfortable double chins, but instead sagged in loose pore-dotted folds — and the rasping, whining note that never left her voice. If there were any single conceivable reason to bad-mouth anyone fool enough to wander within earshot of this woman, Turpin had sometimes thought, it was beyond her powers of self-control to deny herself the pleasure of mentioning it.

Why couldn't the stupid old bag eat a normal diet, get comfortably fat and die young and happy — instead of hanging on until doomsday, griping about everyone and everything? Maybe she'd have kept one of her three husbands if she had!

But all he said aloud was, 'Come now, mother-in-law, you can't say that Sophie is an alcoholic! She does drink more than most people, I imagine, but she's always been highly-strung.'

Mrs Gleewood sniffed. 'And where's your guest?' she snapped. 'That Mr Donald Holtzer, or whatever his name is?'

147

'I believe he — uh — he went out with Lora,' Turpin said, and tensed, his hackles bristling.

'I see,' Mrs Gleewood said. '*I* see! Another scalp, hm?'

'What do you mean?' Bridling — knowing he was expected to, because if he didn't that would ruin her evening. But it was getting harder and harder to fill his designated rôle.

'Scalps,' Mrs Gleewood said with satisfied deliberateness. '*Pubic* scalps. Not yet nineteen, I would remind you, and already she has enough of those to qualify her for a full Indian brave's head-dress. And, while I'm considering the subject of the children you inflicted on my daughter, may I ask what you're going to do about Peter's haemorrhoids?'

Christ! How I'd love to take that scrawny neck and wring it! And I could, I could, I keep myself in good shape and if I just —

He caught himself, barely in time.

Oh, that reeky turd Sheklov! If he weren't here, if I hadn't been compelled to cushion him, I could have rid myself for good of this loathsome, disgusting, incompetent wouldbe matriarch! As soon as I'm shut of him, I'll — I'll. . .

Only he wouldn't. He knew he wouldn't. It would be as hard as curing himself of a habit like smoking or drinking.

He said mildly, 'I'm afraid I don't quite understand.'

Conscious of having won the exchange, Mrs Gleewood sniffed. 'I wish you wouldn't talk while I'm trying to watch TV!' she crowed.

And sat back, delighted with the dialogue.

Meantime, Turpin had something else on his mind. It was — in a paradoxical sense — unreal, because it had been real to him for so long.

Am I going to be exposed?

The afternoon, and early evening until he managed to

148

get away, which he had spent around the reserved area, had already taken on the dimensions of a dream. Because all the time and under no matter what circumstances he had grown used to behaving exactly as someone in his position was expected to, he had obviously to limit his responses to those that a genuinely loyal and committed executive of Energetics General might convincingly display when faced by a crisis of the current magnitude.

In other words, he had to act as though — whatever he might have said, for instance to Clarke — concerning the factually *known* political situation within the country, and hence acknowledging the jealousy between Army and Navy, the constant jockeying for position which never ceased between the various major corporations, always hunting for a larger slice of the Defence Department cake, he had all the right incontrovertible assumptions. Navy would never act against the country's best interests! Corporation X, since it draws down DoD funds, must be staffed by the most loyal of directors! The Security Force, being hand-picked, is unquestionably the court of last resort, and we can safely rely on them to clear up this mess. Of course, one has to be on guard all the time because, as was shown in South-East Asia, Latin America, the Philippines, and God knows where else, the other side is subtle, devious, cunning! But far be it from ME to lose confidence in the wisdom of those who have laid down the precepts by which we live, the experts whose love of freedom has defined the degree to which we, the laymen, and our families, must sacrifice liberty to preserve it.

But at the edge of his awareness, even though he was sure he was acting exactly as he ought to in his position, he could hear what Sheklov had said — about there being alien intelligences who could and conceivably would wipe out modern civilisation. Each time he reviewed his recollection of that incredible statement, it acquired new overtones, new resonances due to his subconscious, new implications pregnant with terror.

149

*And here I am being polite to a stupid old woman
because I have to maintain my cover. Am I crazy?*

The conviction began to grow in his mind.

Yes. Absolutely crazy.

He looked now and then out of the corner of his eye
at the smugly self-satisfied Mrs Gleewood, as though he
were an executioner measuring someone in advance for a
garrotte.

It fitted. It all hung together. Morton Clarke didn't
want to have to believe it, but in the end. . .

He looked, one final time, at the chart he had drawn
on his notepad, linked with arrows: FENELLA CLARKE
to MAGDA HANSEN to DANTY WARD to LORA
TURPIN to LEWIS TURPIN to —

No, it had to stop there. It mustn't go on! Mustn't!
Because somewhere along the line, maybe three stops
from now, the chain of reasoning would close, and the
name would be his own: MORTON CLARKE.

It had to be broken before it was allowed to extend
that far. No one could accuse him of treason.

Slowly, like a martyr hearing the call for his turn at
the Colosseum, he rose from his chair and felt inside his
jacket for his gun. Government issue. Got to be proved
worthy of it. Immediately, before anyone else saw the
connections he had just worked out.

He went into the adjacent room, where Fenella was
watching Channel 8 — no, correction, Channel 9, must
have changed over when the commercials came on. . .

'Hi, Mort honey,' she said. 'Come sit down! What you
been doing all this time?'

'Traitor,' he said.

'What?'

'Traitor! Fucking traitor! Fucking *commie!*'

Bang. Bang. Bang-bang-bang-bang.

The gun was empty. Government issue. Six official
shells expended. Have to account for them. One should

have been enough if he'd come close enough to make it tell.

How to explain to the authorities those five wasted shots?

He sat down beside the chair which her blood was soaking and began to cry, quite unable to think of an excuse.

23

What in hell have I wandered into?

Sheklov's mind rang with that question. But he had no
choice about complying, short of seizing the dashboard
gun and holding it to Magda's side.

At the same time, however, a curious exaltation filled
him. Suppose — just suppose — that by pure chance he
had already stumbled on what he had been looking for:
that 'different attitude of mind' which Bratcheslavsky had
been so insistent about. . .

Where the behaviour of Danty and Magda had relevance
to that alien ship sparkling against the stars, he could not
guess. Nonetheless, he was willing for the time being to
yield to whatever he was told, although he was simultaneously worried about what would happen to his cover as
a Canadian if security's attention was drawn to him.

Hunched forward on the rear seat, speaking almost in
Sheklov's ear, Danty said, 'No, not this turn — go two
more blocks, then make a right. Then we'll come down
our street on the side further from the apartment, and
we'll get a clearer sight of what's happening.'

'What do you *think* is happening?' countered Sheklov
in his best Holtzer manner. 'I can't see any point to this
— '

'Nonsense?' Magda interrupted. 'Don, I've known
Danty a long, long time. Like I told you, he was born
at the wrong end of time. He can feel things that haven't
happened yet.'

'So why didn't he dodge the guy with the knife?'
Sheklov retorted.

152

There was a short silence. Magda turned around in her seat and looked at Danty.

Finally Danty said, 'Because if I hadn't been where they caught up with me, I wouldn't have found out something very important.'

'Danty, what *are* you talking about?' Lora demanded.

Almost in the same moment, Magda said, 'Danty, are you — ?'

'Sure I'm sure!' he snapped. 'It's been getting stronger for several minutes now. I've never had it so strong in my life. Right here, Don, and right again. Around the corner, take it as slow as you can.'

Lora said after a short pause, 'I keep some binocs in the glove compartment — do you want them?'

'Yeah!' Danty sat up straight. 'Mag', pass them to me!'

She pulled open the glove compartment and found them, a cheap Mexican pair in a plastic ever-ready case. He took them and held them ready as Sheklov made the final turn into their home street. At once he let out a hissing breath.

'Look!' he rapped, and set the glasses to his eyes.

Glancing rapidly from the traffic around to the landing, up close to the hoverhalt, from which access to Magda's home was obtained, Sheklov felt a pang of horror. The door was wide open. The window was lighted. Two men were standing guard, suspiciously eyeing passengers descending from a recently-arrived hovercar, and apparently giving off some sort of repellent aura, because these passengers were keeping their distance.

Also — and this gave him an excuse to drive very slowly — two large cars were illegally parked against the kerb instead of in parking-bays.

'Pigs?' Lora said, her voice quavering.

'Not pigs,' Danty said, staring through the glasses. 'Security Force. Mag', I'm afraid you've lost your home.'

'What do you mean?' Sheklov snapped. 'I don't know what those security men — if they *are* security men — I

153

don't know what they're doing in your apartment, but surely you don't mean that!'

'Don't mean it?' Danty repeated, lowering the binocs now that they had passed the building and it was impossible to see the landing where the men stood guard. 'Tell him, Mag' baby.'

She was sitting very still, face white, eyes staring straight ahead. But her hands were folded over so that her nails were deep in her palms.

'He's right,' she said in a dead voice. 'Pigs you can take. Once the sexies hit you, you're done for.'

'Sexies?' Sheklov echoed, and caught himself, realising that the term stood for 'security execs'.

'But this is crazy!' Lora burst out. 'Hell! You can't just cave in! What about — ?' With a snap of her fingers. 'Hey! My father! He has lots of pull! He'll get 'em off your backs. Just let me get to a phone and tell him what's to be done.'

She was so agitated, she was reaching for the door-handle.

But Danty had completely ignored the interruption. He was looking solely at Magda.

'Well?' he said. 'I'm sorry, you know — more sorry than I can say. Not that that does any good.'

'No.' Magda stirred, as though from a period of deep meditation, and helped herself to another cigarette. 'No, it doesn't do any good. All right, the avalanche has begun. I guess I half-expected it. You're in charge.'

The door-bell sounded. Turpin, glad of the interruption, rose from his chair with alacrity.

'Sit down!' Mrs Gleewood rasped. '*You* don't have to answer the door! What do you keep Estelle for?'

'It's Estelle's evening off,' Turpin said with satisfaction. 'Sunday, remember? Also Peter is out, Lora is out, and Sophie is drunk. You said so yourself. So unless you propose to go and answer — ?'

She glowered at him and then stared firmly at the TV again.

He went to the panel by the door of the living-room where the intercom was, and pressed the answer button to activate the mike.

'Yes, who is it?'

'Is that Mr Turpin personally?' a cold strange voice inquired.

'Ah — yes.' Butterflies began to perform in Turpin's belly.

'My name is Thorpe, Eric Thorpe. Security force. May I see you for a moment?'

Oh, Christ...

But habit made him impervious, on the surface, to even shocks like that one. He said, 'Surely!' In a tone as cheerful as though he really were pleased to be distracted from the company of his mother-in-law. 'I'll be with you in just a second.'

Crossing the hall, ignoring the call Mrs Gleewood hurled after him — wanting to be told who the visitor was — he reviewed a hundred possibilities in ten seconds, and found that he liked none of them. Pray that his hints to Clarke, out at the reserved area, had borne fruit...

He checked, through the spy remotes that there was indeed no one but this single man in the elevator, and opened the door on a security stop.

'I'd like to see your redbook, if you don't — ' he began, but Thorpe had anticipated the request and was already holding it up so it could be read through the narrow gap. Yes, he was who he said he was, and moreover he held the rank of substantive warden.

'Come in,' Turpin muttered. 'We'll use my den — it's bug-free.'

He led the way; offered a drink — refused — and a cigarette, which was accepted. Sat down, and to his dismay found he had to put his hands together to stop them shaking.

155

'Well, what can I do for you?' he said. His voice at least sounded under control. 'I guess it's about this affair at the reserved area, hm?'

'Indirectly.' Thorpe was a pale man, with deep-set eyes surrounded by dark rings, as though he lived on far too little sleep and had done for years. Like all SF executives, he wore unremarkable and inexpensive clothes: tonight, in dark green. 'I believe you talked for some while with one of my brother officers, didn't you?'

'Morton Clarke?'

'Yes.'

'Well, I imagine we must have talked, on and off, over a period of — let's see — three hours. Why?'

'About. . . ?'

'Well, the alarming discovery that had been made,' Turpin said. 'And the implications. Wasn't that obvious?'

Thorpe looked down at his involuntary host's hands, as though scrutinising them for signs of anxiety. He said, in a matter-of-fact tone, 'Of course. And I believe you are slightly acquainted with a young black named Danty Ward?'

What the hell is this leading up to?

Turpin said as levelly as he could, 'Acquainted would be an exaggeration. I met him last night, because my daughter invited him to our party, and one can hardly refuse his own daughter's guests admission. Why? Has he done something?'

Thorpe ignored that question. He continued, 'How long has your daughter known this — uh — person?'

'I've no idea,' Turpin snapped.

'Are you also acquainted with a woman going by the name of Mrs Magda Hansen?'

'Not that I can recall,' Turpin said, blinking.

'Do you know a Mrs Avice Donnelly?'

'You mean Fred Donnelly's wife — our plant security chief? Well, naturally I do! But only slightly. Look!' He sat forward. 'Will you tell me what this is about?'

Thorpe raised his eyes and met Turpin's and locked with them.

'Sabotage. Subversion. Murder. Treason. That's what it's about, Mr Turpin. It would appear that Morton Clarke has been given what we presume to be a post-hypnotic order to kill his wife, and has done so.'

'*What?*'

'Yes, I'm afraid that's apparently the case.' Like a good security man, Thorpe always qualified assertions of that order. 'Have you any idea where your daughter is?'

'I — uh — *no!*' Turpin felt sweat breaking out all over his body.

'Or Danty Ward?'

'Hell, of course not!'

'I see.' Thorpe cogitated a moment, and then rose. 'Well, I'm afraid I'm going to have to ask you to come with me, Mr Turpin. To avoid the possibility of embarrassing you, of course, I came alone, but I should point out that everything we say can be overheard by colleagues of mine waiting in a car below, and I would counsel you not to decline, or it will become essential to escort you away under guard. Shall we go?'

'Night-riding,' Danty said suddenly. 'Head north. Don't stop at the first or second gas-station we pass, but call at the one by the superway entrance on Sixtieth. Fill up there.'

'Now just a second!' Sheklov exploded.

'Don't argue,' Magda said. 'Do as you're told.' And, with a movement as quick as a striking snake, she snatched the dashboard gun from its socket and flipped off the safety-catch, levelling it at Sheklov.

'Oh, shit, Magda!' Danty exclaimed. 'No need for that! Put it down, will you?'

'But —'

In the rear-view mirror Sheklov caught a glimpse of Lora, face perfectly white, knuckles pressed to her teeth

157

as though to suppress a scream. He felt pretty much like screaming himself.

'No buts!' Danty said angrily. 'I mean, Don here wouldn't want it to be known that he's Russian, would he? Say! What's your real name, by the way? Ivan? Yuri? Nikita?'

24

There was a brief terrible instant during which Sheklov found himself insanely wishing that he believed in a personal god who could be trusted to provide on-the-spot salvation for his worshippers.

How long has he known? And, worse yet:

Who has he told?

He continued to go through the right motions and drive the car, mechanically, like a robot: red light, slow down; green, step on the gas; miss that idiot pulling out from that parking-bay without looking... But that had nothing to do with his conscious mind. It was all automatic.

'I think you're out of your skull,' he husked at last. 'I'm going to find a parking-bay and get out, and leave you to your — your mad fantasies!'

'*Russian?*' Lora said, as though the word had been in her throat for a short eternity, building up pressure until now it came blasting out like the plug of semi-solid magma which chokes the crater of a volcano until it erupts.

'Yes, of course!' Danty snapped. 'Either that, or perhaps Polish, Hungarian, Czech — no, my guess is Russian. Well, Don?'

'You're insane! You're hallucinating or something!' But Sheklov's mouth was so dry he could barely speak.

'Maybe you were right after all, Mag',' Danty sighed. 'Okay, put the gun back on him, but keep it well out of sight. He's missed death by inches once in the past few days, when he came ashore. And that would have spread him kind of thin and all over everywhere, so — '

'Look out!' Magda exclaimed, and seized the wheel just in time, twisting it to the left and then straightening out. Lora let go a cry of alarm. Sheklov had nearly crashed into the back of a truck.

'That got to him,' Danty said softly. 'Don, baby, didn't you know the site was turned off when you came ashore? Didn't you know that if it hadn't been the submarine would have been blasted less than a mile away? They weren't so careful when they left as when they approached.'

'You just figured that out?' Magda said, and in the same breath added, 'Pull over, Don. You're not in a fit state to drive. You're shaking so much. I'll take the wheel as soon as you can put us in a parking-bay — ah, there's one now.'

Dumb, Sheklov nosed the car into it.

'Well, it's how it had to be,' Danty said. 'I felt something *bad* on the way. And I can't think of any other disaster that fits the picture — No, Don! Don't get out! Slide towards Magda and let her climb over you!'

Sheklov, numb, withdrew his hand from the door-handle and obeyed.

As Magda took the controls: 'So that's the way I see it. If the site hadn't been turned off, the sub would have registered on the detectors, and — pow.'

'But he's been staying right in our apartment!' Lora cried. She was having to clamp her jaw to stop her teeth chattering. 'A Russian! A spy!'

'You recommended the gas-station on Sixtieth, didn't you?' Magda said, glancing at the dash. 'Oh, shit! Lora! *Lora!* Stop your snivelling and tell me which of these damned dials is the gas-gauge!'

'Uh. . . ' Wiping her eyes on her sleeve. 'Doesn't have a dial. It's sonic.'

'Just say to fill up the tank,' Danty snapped. 'Night-riders usually do.'

'Yeah.' Magda slowed to make the turn on to Sixtieth, a right. 'But why the hell did you leave the site turned off?'

'I guess. . . ' Danty swallowed hard. 'I guess so that this would happen. So that we'd be here, now, in this mess.'

'Gas-station!' Magda said unnecessarily; it was blazing with light and huge mobile advertising figures, spotlighted, filled with helium, and tugged into a weird non-stop parody of a dance by fine wires attached to cams on electric motors, signalled drivers to pull in. 'Don, you hold your tongue and behave yourself, hm? And you, Lora!'

'No! Let me out!' Lora cried, and as the car swung close to the side of the road, in order to enter the gas-station, tried to snatch at the door-handle.

Danty stopped her, his dark hand closing over her mouth and his full strength forcing her back against the seat.

'I may only have one hand right now,' he said in a voice as cold as a Siberian winter, 'but if I have to I'll strangle you. Is that understood?'

For a moment Sheklov thought she was going to fight back; her fists curled over and her eyes widened in a look of fury. Then, abruptly, she yielded, and went limp. When he took his hand away, she stared at Danty with a kind of adoration, as though this were the first time in her life that someone had given her an order meant to be obeyed — and she liked the novel sensation.

'Full, please!' Magda called as they drew up to the pumps.

'Full it is!' came the reply over the remote speakers.

'I. . . ' Sheklov licked his lips. 'I meant to ask someone: why do you lay your gas-stations out this way, with the attendants in those high glass booths?'

'Robbery,' Magda said. 'Maybe the risk of sabotage, too. There was a time a few years ago, when I was in my teens, when gas-stations were closing down all over. They made such a lovely show when someone tossed a Molotov cocktail at the pumps.'

Cash-drawer. Credit card. Usual routine. During it, Sheklov noticed that Danty was tensing and biting his lower lip. Then, as soon as the card came back and they were leaving the station, he spoke up.

'I just figured out how they got on to us.'

'You and me, you mean?' Magda said, spotting a gap in the traffic and accelerating violently towards it. 'So, how?'

'A cat called Rollins — get on the superway as soon as you can, hm? — gave me a ride back to Cowville. We stopped for gas and a suspicious pig came and checked the governor on his car. A Banshee. Thought it had been sorted out. I guess he would have filed a report. He looked at my redbook.'

'Ah-hah. And the sexies got to the tape of the report, hm? Yes, that fits. So this time wherever we go, we go for good.'

'I still think you're crazy — 'Sheklov began, but Danty cut him short.

'Look, Ivan or whatever your real name is! Get this into your head, will you? I was there on the beach when you came ashore. I saw you get into Turpin's car — '

'What?' From Lora, a shrill-edged cry of horror.

'Yeah, you heard!' Danty snapped. 'Your dad's car! I saw it again in the garage under the tower you live in. Recognised the licence number, so don't give me any shit! Like I was saying, Ivan! Do you want that lot to come out when they catch up with me and start feeding me interrogation drugs?'

Ahead, the superway access point loomed, brilliant with neon strips forming arrows and the letter N for northbound. Sheklov caught a brief glimpse of the name of some city, and a distance, but failed to read them clearly.

'You're in the laughing seat,' Magda said sourly, swinging into the traffic on the superway. As ever, there was a vast horde of it; this was about the time — midnight — when the night-riders took to the road. Here and there a heavy truck lumbered along in the slow lanes, and the drivers of private cars blasted their horns to register their opinion that all trucks should be forbidden these roads.

'Huh?' Danty said. 'Oh, you mean what I was saying a few hours ago, I guess. Like about getting out?'

'Yeah.'

'I meant it,' Danty said after a pause. 'But. . . Well, tell Ivan here what happens to someone when the sexies put the knife in.'

'Oh, life simply stops being worth living,' Magda said. 'Even if they don't convict you of anything, the fact that you're under suspicion gets around. They have computer-to-computer links, you know' — with a glance at Sheklov beside her — 'for absolutely everything you may want to do. Your credit rating goes first, and your cards are cancelled, and as you probably know carrying cash in this country is a bad idea. Has been since God knows when. Before Danty was born, certainly.'

'Right,' Danty agreed.

'Robbery again?' Sheklov hazarded. He was on the verge of caving in; these people took it so matter-of-factly that he was Russian, and it didn't trouble them at all — only the attention of the Security Force was on their minds.

'Not just that — I mean, not just the risk of *being* robbed,' Magda said. Now, already, at the high speeds permitted on the superway, the city was dwindling and the dark shell of the night was closing them in. 'More the automatic assumption that if you're carrying more than like fifty bucks — peanuts! -- you're the thief. Lose your credit rating, you might as well be bankrupt. After, that, of course, if you have a job, they make sure your employers find out. Then your landlord; that's the usual

163

order. If you're married, your spouse, and particularly your kids, if they're over say eight or ten years old. I had a client once who came to me because her son, who was thirteen, had heard his father was under suspicion by the sexies, and wanted her to run away with him where Dad couldn't find them, then inform on him to the pigs.'

'The price of liberty is eternal vigilance,' Danty said, and made the quotation downright obscene.

'Is this — is this so literally true that you're running out on your home?' Sheklov said in a bewildered tone, no longer sure whether he was Holtzer or himself.

'And our country, if we can make it,' Danty said. 'Like Magda just told you, once the searchlight turns on you, life stops being worth living. Mag'!'

'Yes?'

'I'm sorry. Truly I am. If I'd been any better at my thing, I'd have kept you from getting involved — '

'Oh, zip it up,' Magda cut in wearily. 'I guess you were right when you talked to me earlier on. I don't have anything worth staying for. Hell, it's got to where if I order a book I'm interested in through the mail, a pig shows up the day after it's delivered asking why I wanted it.'

'Yeah,' Danty said. 'And. . . Well, if it's any consolation, I feel — beyond any doubt — that this is a *right* thing to do. It leads somewhere. It does something terribly important which I can't understand. But I'm sure, I'm *convinced* it does it!'

Sheklov, listening, felt a renewal of that unaccountable exaltation which had struck him on the way into Cowville.

'Where are we going?' Lora said faintly.

'Canada,' Danty said. 'Put you off a hundred miles or so from here, if you like. If you promise not to set the sexies on us, or the pigs.'

'Canada?' Sheklov snapped, before Lora could answer. 'But it's not as simple as — '

'The grapevine tells you where you can still get across,'

164

Magda broke in. 'We know a couple of places. Dodgy, but with Danty to take care of us, we'll make it. And of course the moment you set foot on Canadian soil, they'd die rather than turn you back. . . '

'I don't want to be put out,' Lora said abruptly. Danty and Sheklov looked at her hard.

'No,' she emphasised. 'If it's true that — that my father brought a Russian agent into. . . ? ' It turned into a question, and died away. Danty nodded vigorously.

'Whatever Ivan says,' he insisted.

'Then he lied to me all my life,' Lora whispered. 'I don't want to see him again as long as I live. And that's not crazy talk. I'm cold sober again, and I *mean* it.'

In which case. . .

Sheklov felt as though he was going over the edge of a cliff into deep, icy water. But he said, 'My name isn't Ivan. It's Vassily.'

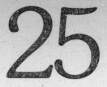

Lora huddled away into the corner of the rear seat and could be heard faintly crying — not sobbing, simply snuffling. Headlights on the other half of the road shot towards them like tracer-bullets.

Sheklov thought: *Regarding success and failure alike. . .*

Well, at the moment he was compelled to, whether or not he had achieved detachment. Because he had absolutely no inkling which had overtaken him. Either he had failed, spectacularly and monstrously, and was going to have to kill himself and his companions in order to avoid exposure of Turpin, or else he had succeeded in some manner he did not understand.

Danty knew I was due to come ashore. He was there when I arrived, watching me. He saw Turpin's car take me away.

He had turned off the site. How did he know the way to do it safely? Turpin said he would hardly dare to try the job without a schematic.

He appeared to be claiming that he foresaw the submarine being blown up if the site were not switched off. Then he left it switched off, thereby ensuring — he said as much — that we would be here, in this mess.

The whole thing is crazy! And so am I!

Yet, behind all these surface thoughts, there was a kind of echo: recollection of what Magda had said, twice.

'Danty was born at the wrong end of time.'

A joking comment! Must be! But it had a — a ring to it. An overtone. Some all-important hidden meaning. Tantalising, like having a word on the tip of your tongue and being unable to utter it.

There had been silence in the car, except for Lora's soft weeping, for many miles. It was as though his admission concerning his identity had been a minor climax in the course of events, and, it being passed, Danty was content to wait for some new pattern to develop. Magda, at the wheel, was patently too depressed to talk; she wore an expression of unspeakable sadness, revealed flick-flick-flick by the on-coming headlamps.

From all the various directions in which his mind had been scattered, Sheklov forcibly pulled himself back together. He reviewed what had to be said; having organised it, he spoke.

'Danty!'

'Yes?'

'I probably don't need to tell you that this — this talent of yours has completely blown my mind. I don't believe it, but I've been driven to accept it.'

'That figures,' Danty said dryly, and added: '*Vassily!* By the way, what kind of a name is that? Is it Russian?'

'Yes. Though it was Greek originally. Funny, you know!' Sheklov gave a short harsh laugh. 'It means "king". Not the ideal name for a good third-generation Party man.'

'But you're not one,' Danty said.

'I — ' Sheklov began, and broke off. After a moment, he admitted, 'No, in some ways I guess not.'

'You're too independent,' Danty said with assurance. 'Like Magda, or me, come to that. You can quote the *Gita*, for example, as though you took it seriously. My guess would be you have it by heart.'

'When you wormed that out of me, I almost had a heart-attack,' Sheklov said. *Was it only last night? It feels like a year ago!* But that was a good illusion to be under. It lent the comforting impression of distance in time to his borderline panic. He didn't want to be reminded right

167

now that he was capable of panic. He had to keep his mind at its finest pitch, to reason out and plan this ridiculous journey they were committed to.

'Yes, I'm sorry about that,' Danty muttered. 'But . . . Well, this talent of mine. I'll try and explain how it works, as far as I understand it myself — which isn't very well.' He hunched forward and rested his unhurt arm on the back of Sheklov's seat, staring past him at the cars on the superway.

'Since I was — oh — sixteen, seventeen, I guess, now and then I've felt a funny pressure at the back of my head, a sensation that belongs in the same group with hunger and thirst, because it means I have to do something to satisfy it. It makes me grope around like a blind man, or sometimes just wander from one place to another until I feel the pressure fading a little and I realise I'm on the right track. Now and then I can tell quite clearly that I have to be at some special place at some special time. Like the morning of your arrival. I knew a direction I had to go in, I knew I'd recognise the spot when I reached it.'

'And you knew how to shut down the site,' Sheklov said, marvelling.

'That was the same process,' Danty said. 'I got through the fences around the site by — by picturing an action in my mind and waiting to find out whether the pressure in my head got better or worse. Then I did the same thing with the lock on the control bunker, and then with the switches. I was asking this talent of mine, 'Is it safe to close this one? Is it safe to close that one?' And all the time I knew I had to get this right, because otherwise there was going to be a great crashing disaster. Like I told you, I figured out later that the sub which put you ashore would have triggered the detectors.'

'Thank you,' Sheklov said soberly. '*I* wouldn't have cared to be a mile from the explosion of one of those missiles.'

'Nor would I,' Danty said, with his regular crooked

168

smile. 'And then there's one other thing about my talent. I can sense, in the same general way, how to — to inveigle people into doing things they didn't intend to. I can sort of time words which prompt them to react.'

'Like making me quote the *Gita*.'

'Right. I can't pull the trick all the time, only when something has built up the pressure in my head to a particular pitch. When I'm sensing something terribly important.' Danty passed his hand across his eyes. 'And I never felt anything a fraction as important as — as you.'

'How do you feel about me, then?' Sheklov countered.

'It's hard to describe. Say huge. Say vast. Say colossal. You still aren't within miles of hitting the idea. It's like looking up into the sky and thinking yourself into a state where you can actually understand a million light-years. Feeling in your guts a gulf that takes light all that time to crawl across. Something that makes the whole of history, the whole story of life on Earth, the age of the Earth itself, *tiny!*'

A shiver trembled down Sheklov's spine. He began to dare to think that he might, just *might*, have succeeded in his mission. He still didn't see how, but the possibility was now credible.

Magda, unexpectedly, spoke up. She said, 'Danty, what point of the border should we make for?'

'I'm still not quite clear on that,' Danty said. 'Keep heading north, that's all. I should be able to tell you in a little while what the safest zone would be.'

'Are we going to keep driving through the day, or lie up somewhere, or what?'

'Now that's odd,' Danty said, biting his lip. 'I was thinking we ought to worry about this car, because obviously the licence number can be recognised, and you'd expect that if Lora doesn't show at home it'll be reported. But I have this absolute conviction that we're safe if we go on driving. I have this crazy idea that even if the car has been — oh — reported stolen, say, it's not

169

going to be taken seriously.' He hesitated. 'And I can only think of one explanation for that.'

'What?' Magda demanded.

'Well. . .' Danty licked his lips. 'I think because the person who would report it is Turpin, and he's in trouble.'

He glanced reflexively at Lora, in case she had heard. But she was asleep.

Sheklov thought: *Bad trouble? Because it would be a catastrophe for the whole world if he were caught.*

'Is Turpin one of yours?' Magda asked, with a sidelong glance at Sheklov. When he didn't answer, she answered for herself. 'I guess he must be, since he collected you from the submarine.'

'What's the use of denying it?' Sheklov said wearily. 'Yes, he is. And he's one of the greatest heroes in history and he's never going to get credit for it.'

'He will one day,' Danty said.

'What?'

'I know what you mean,' Danty murmured. 'I've often wondered how the world had stayed in one piece, and I just saw a good reason. He told you about all the missiles, the radar, and that kind of stuff — right?'

'Yes.'

'Thank God somebody did,' Danty said, and Magda nodded.

Are these people never going to stop amazing me? Sheklov thought. He said curiously, 'Tell me something, will you? How do you feel about — about *me?*'

'As a Russian agent?' Danty suggested, and on Sheklov's hesitant nod gave a shrug. 'Oh, as a brave man, I guess. Dedicated. You'd have to be. And clever. But if you mean as a — a foreigner, a communist, all the other things, then. . .'

'Lucky,' Magda said.

'I don't get that,' Sheklov said. 'How, lucky?'

'Well, because you still have somewhere to go,' Magda said. 'That's as near as I can define what I mean. Look at

170

us here in this country. We're in the same sort of mess
as the Romans were once, and the Spanish, and God
knows who else. We've been at the top of the heap, and
now there's no choice except either to run like hell to
stay where we are, never getting any place else, or to start
the long slide down. Me, I think we started down years
ago. We've been the richest country in the world, we've
been the most powerful, we've been the most influential,
and — same as always — we got used to it. We got blasé.
Because we couldn't climb any higher, we stopped being
able to advance. There hasn't been anything genuinely
new in the States for years and years, just changes rung
on what we already had. But of course we were afraid of
being overtaken. So we drifted into this mess we're in
right now, where we care more about our own selfishness
and greed than we do about anyone or anything else.
What's a good career for a bright young man these days?
Why, the security force — or a tidy slot in the hierarchy
of Energetics General — or something of that kind. Where
are our poets, our musicians, our inventors? They've turned reb! And got stamped on!' She glanced at him. 'Aren't
I right?'

'Being "on top" isn't the important thing,' Sheklov
said.

'Of course not,' Magda snapped. 'If it were, we'd feel
satisfied. We'd feel — oh — fulfilled!'

'And we don't,' Danty said. 'Say, Vassily! There's one
thing you haven't told us yet, and I have this impression
that it's the most crucial point of all. Why in the world
did they decide to risk sending you to the States? I mean,
if Turpin is one of your agents, he must have been here
for years — '

'Twenty-five,' Sheklov said.

'That long? Hmm! Yes, it figures. And he can't be the
only one, right?'

'No, he's not.'

'So why did they have to send you? I mean, you could

171

have walked straight into the jaws of the sexies, couldn't you? Lots of practice has made them very good at their job.'

Sheklov thought for a long moment.
Then he told them.

26

After that there seemed to be very little left to say. The car hummed onward into the night. Clouds were closing in ahead of them; it felt as though the familiar prospect of the stars was being shut away. Sheklov, conscious of having long ago passed the point of no return, was resigned to letting happen what would.

And Danty, having heard the story in full, sank back in his seat with a ferocious scowl of concentration and said nothing for so long that eventually Sheklov dozed.

He was awoken at last by Magda's voice.

'I'm worn out!' she said loudly. 'It's nearly dawn.'

'Then I guess I'd better take the wheel again,' Sheklov said. 'Danty can't drive one-handed, and' — with a glance behind him, blinking to clear sleep from his eyes — 'Lora's still asleep, isn't she?'

'Looks like it,' Danty said. 'I'd take my turn if I could — but this arm's stiffening up pretty bad. Mag', can we like pull in for breakfast? I'd like to get to a washroom and change the dressing on this cut.' He checked, seeming to be struck by an idea. 'Say! Make the left branch at the next interchange, will you? I'm getting it clearer in my head now. We have to shoot for the border in North Dakota some place. I'll know it when I see it.'

'Service zone four miles,' Magda read from a sign. 'That must be after the next interchange, then. Will do. . . By the way, how are you feeling?'

'As though that crack on the head loosened my brains,' Danty said with a shrug. 'But I'll live.'

Properly roused from sleep now, Sheklov looked out

at the morning as it spread across the vast net of the superway. A web spun by an inconceivable spider, a mesh of concrete offering the illusion of freedom to go, yet turning you back whenever you approached the limits you must not exceed. . .

Yes. A metaphor of the country. Perhaps of the human condition. Horrible!

All his doubts stormed back into his mind. For a brief instant he was able to imagine that he had dreamed his admissions of last night; then Danty said, 'Vassily, how are you?' And he knew they had been real.

'As well as can be expected,' Sheklov said with ghoulish humour.

'That goes for all of us.' He rubbed his eyes. 'Mag', I've only been dozing, not completely asleep. I've been working it out. North Dakota, like I said. If we go over as a party, we're likely to be recognised. I don't know why or how. I only feel it. I'm still trying to sort that out. But something else keeps getting in the way. Vassily, you did say, didn't you, that the aliens showed pictures of Earth?'

'Nine still pictures,' Sheklov said.

'Could you — well — maybe draw them for me?'

'I guess so,' Sheklov answered after a moment for thought. 'I looked at the photographs often enough. Might not get the details right, but in principle they'd be correct.'

'Fine,' Danty said, and gave his crooked smile. 'Over breakfast I'll take you up on it. Mag', isn't that the service zone up ahead?'

The restaurant of the service zone was nearly empty. Only a couple of incurious long-distance truck-drivers glanced at them as they entered. Having collected coffee and food from the counter, they sat down around a table isolated in the centre of the room and Danty produced a stack of paper serviettes.

'Okay, Vassily, shoot,' he said, and sat back, sipping

174

his coffee.

'What are you doing?' Lora said dispiritedly. She had hardly seemed to be awake when she stumbled from the car; now she sat with eyes red, hair tangled, displaying every sign of exhaustion, as though she had been the one who had to drive through the night. Magda, by contrast, seemed hardly affected. Pale, perhaps, but calm-faced and moving without obvious signs of fatigue.

'Drawing,' Sheklov said, unclipping a ballpen from his pocket. He added, reaching for the first of the pile of white serviettes, 'And I'm not very good at it. But I'll do what I can.'

He captioned each drawing as he completed it with quick sure strokes; he had studied these enigmatic pictures — or at least the photos of them brought back from Pluto's orbit, smeared a little with free-space cosmic radiation, but with pretty good detail surviving — and they were branded on his memory. Of course, pen-sketches like these were hard to make clear. He added a caption to each, summarising what the experts had deduced about them.

Finally, when the others had finished their food, he gestured for a space to be cleared and laid them out in sequence in front of Danty.

'This first one is obviously a view of our galaxy,' he said. 'One can see the spiral arms. Then there's a clear view of the alien ship, which is a plain ovoid, but quite unlike anything of ours, so it's unmistakable. Then there's a view of the sun from a long way out in space — from about where the alien ship is orbiting, in fact. You can be certain of that because the constellations in the background match. I don't know astronomy well enough to do more than dot them in. Then there's a view of Earth, here; the continents are perfectly recognisable, though they're partly masked by cloud, as though the aliens are working from a particular picture.

'After that, there's a human-built rocket, possibly a satellite-launcher, possibly one of our own ships that made

175

the Pluto trip first. That's interesting; apparently the engineers have spotted some detail-refinements in the design, and they seem promising. It's rather as though you were to try and draw a Model T from memory and absent-mindedly make it look like a much more recent make of car.

'Then there's this. An explosion. Notice it's centred on the United States. And in the original — I'm afraid I haven't drawn this very well — in the actual picture you can see it's nuclear. The likeliest explanation, the one which frightens us so much, and drove my superiors to send me here, is that it's a strike by the aliens.'

Magda was staring, fascinated, although Lora was leaning back in her chair with her eyes half-closed and Danty was bestowing only casual glances on each successive picture. Suddenly irritated by his lack of interest, Sheklov let his tone grow sharper.

'Next is this one, a plain circle. That puzzled us terribly. But the logical conclusion is that it's the Earth again, wiped out by clouds of dust and smoke. Because here . . .' He reached for the last two drawings.

'This is fire. No mistake about it. Something burning violently. And last of all there's — this.'

He laid down the caveman picture, the figure draped in skins waving a stone axe. And sat back.

There was a dead silence.

Eventually Danty picked up the drawings, like Magda gathering her tarot cards, and reversed them. He laid them out again on the table in the opposite order, turning each around as he set it down so as to be the correct way up from Sheklov's viewpoint the other side of the table.

'No,' he said. '*This* way.'

For a long moment Sheklov stared at them. Then he raised his eyes to Danty's calm, amused face.

'Are you — sure?' he said huskily.

'As sure as I am that we're going to find a way over

the border, dodge the guards, dodge the mines, get to safety. And that's close to one hundred per cent. I only got one life, Vassily, and I'm fond of it in spite of everything.'

Sheklov sat frozen. In his mind he could hear words, as clear as though someone were uttering them aloud:

The last shall be first, and the first. . .

'Right,' Danty said with a chuckle. 'Let's move on.'

27

'But he was wrong,' Bratcheslavsky murmured, taking
from its pack yet another of his endless series of *papyrosi*
and bending its cardboard tube to a right angle prepara-
tory to lighting it at the flame of the hanging brass lamp
which swung from the centre of the small room's white
ceiling.

Standing by the window which gave such a fine view
of the city of Alma-Ata, shrouded at the moment in the
pale grey mists of early evening, Sheklov said without
looking around, 'Of course he wasn't. He was simply
lying.'

He sighed and helped himself to a cigarette from the
pack, then came to join Bratcheslavsky on the cushions
piled here and there across the floor, not randomly but
with the imprecise symmetry of a Japanese sand-garden.

'But you knew the whole border was heavily beset
with patrols. And the further the frontier zone from a
major city and major roads — in North Dakota, for example, where you were heading for — the more it's likely to
be infested with these "private" defence forces. You
must have realised that!'

'Naturally I did.' Savouring the aromatic tobacco,
Sheklov let a puff of smoke drift into the updraught
from the lamp-flame. Glints of light flashed on its sup-
porting chains.

'And you didn't try and argue with him? Not at all?'

'I was past the stage of disbelieving him,' Sheklov said
after a short pause. 'I'd been convinced, long before, that
he was possessed of a talent I'd barely dreamed of.'

'And it's lost!' Bratcheslavsky barked, jumping to his feet in the first access of honest rage Sheklov had ever seen from him. 'When I think what use we could have made of him — *ach!*'

Sheklov remained squatting on his cushions, gazing up at the old man who had been his mentor for so long, seeing him with curiously different eyes. He felt that his mission, brief as it had been, had altered him. Aged him? Yes, possibly it was only that. . . yet he felt it reached deeper into his personality. He felt not simply that he had crammed a great many years into the space of a few weeks, but also that he'd been educated.

Educated? Enlightened? No, that still wasn't the precise turn of phrase he was after. He cogitated, and suddenly he had it.

Made more wise.

Yes. Yes, exactly. He had had his entire perspective on the world, the human condition, the universe, turned upside-down — and the new version was no less real than the traditional one. He was in the predicament of a savage shown a mirror for the first time, who has painfully to learn the truth that a man's right hand reflected in a mirror is his left.

But all that had been present in his mind while he was in Canada, arranging his onward journey to Russia with the aid and connivance of the company whose representative he had nominally been during his time in the States. So now it had flashed back to his awareness in less than the blink of an eye, and Bratcheslavsky was still talking.

'Not only that, what's more! Not just a man with a talent we'd give our eye-teeth to control! But very likely Turpin too, who's been a mainstay of human survival for a quarter of a century!'

'But they don't suspect him of being an agent, do they?' Sheklov demanded. 'Only of — uh — contact with subversives.'

'There's too damned good a chance of his being tried

179

for treason.' Curtly. 'Navy has jumped into the mess with both feet, and every corporation that's jealous of Energetics General is demanding a chance to take over the defence contracts, and all in all you never saw anything more like the Byzantine Empire in your life! I wouldn't bet against the possibility of the president being deposed, I swear I wouldn't!'

'By an Army coup?'

'Yes, of course. It's inevitable, you know, once you let the armed forces take over key organs of your government. Simply because they can impose rigid discipline on their members, whereas the loose inchoate mass of the public is uncontrollable, they're bound to wind up giving the orders. Didn't we come perilously close to it ourselves a couple of times? And it wasn't good judgment that saved us, only luck.'

Bratcheslavsky tore the cigarette from his mouth and gave it a searing glare; he had bitten completely through its cardboard tube. Tossing it into a sandbowl with an oath, he lit another.

'But surely, even if we do lose Turpin,' Sheklov countered, 'this process will bear out what Marxism has always prophesied: the dissolution of the capitalist state into a brutal internal power-struggle. There'll be so many factions we'll be able to feed in spies, saboteurs, subversives, anyone we choose. All we'll have to do is identify those of the competing parties which are prepared to sell out in order to do down their rivals. Ten years of that, and America will never be a menace to the world again.'

'You're an optimist these days,' Bratcheslavsky grunted.

'I have good reason. I found things over there I wasn't expecting, would have assumed not to exist. Admittedly, they are neither officially admitted nor properly understood, but they exist, and I'm here because they do.'

He drew a deep breath.

'Look! My stay there was measured in days. I don't

180

believe I could have run across what I did unless these — these virtues and talents are widespread. Just consider.' He raised a finger. 'First, I encountered someone with a talent we'd never imagined to be real, only it *was* real and I had proof. What's more, he. . . Well, it's an unfashionable virtue, but it is one.'

'Self-sacrifice,' Bratcheslavsky said.

'Yes.'

There was a long cold pause. During it Sheklov felt himself carried back in space and time, to the train he had taken over the Canadian border on Danty's instructions. None of them had the mind to question his orders by that stage. No one suspected the genuineness of his Canadian passport; for him it had been easy. For Lora and Magda, somewhat harder. . . but there was a well-established underground railway into Canada, had been for over a generation, and it had been surprisingly simple to obtain advice and even a guide. (Of course he'd only heard the details afterwards.)

For Danty, though. . .

He'd looked out of the train's window, and seen that car racing down one of the blocked stub-ends of dirt road heading north, and behind a mask of trees he'd seen that rose of flame. Just for a moment, a second or two.

Why? *Why?* Merely so as to ensure that when his train was checked by the border-guards, most of them would have been diverted to investigate the explosion? It was far too high a price!

But he continued, raising another finger. 'And I met Magda, who in spite of the stifling effects of public conformism had worked out, from the inside, the true historical analogies for her country's predicament. And' — a third finger — 'Lora, who behaved in this crazy manner and nonetheless was ready to abandon her old life for good and all, simply because she'd discovered that her father had lied to her since she was born. That hatred of hypocrisy is a healthy sign. . . Did you bring them out safely, by the way? I didn't hear.'

'Yes, it was confirmed this morning. They wanted to stay in Canada, I'm afraid, but of course we couldn't allow that, not since they both knew about you and Turpin. But don't worry — we'll make them comfortable and take care of them.'

'Fine,' Sheklov said dispiritedly, and stubbed his cigarette in the sandbowl. 'Tell me something,' he added after a moment. 'Why do you think Danty did it?'

'I can only guess,' Bratcheslavsky said. 'Still, it'll be an enlightened guess. I'm an old man, and I've been through so much in one lifetime I seem to have summed up whole generations of human experience. Not about the material world, but about the spiritual world. The material world is run by people like those' — he jerked his head at the door of the room, through which they were soon going to have to pass in order to explain something vitally significant to people who would have no conception of its true importance — 'who are merely efficient. Good at ruling, good at directing, good at ordering other people about. That wasn't Danty's talent. His was for influencing people, encouraging them, not an engineer's talent, but an artist's.'

'Yes,' Sheklov said, almost surprised.

'You envy him that gift, don't you?'

'I . . . Yes, I do.'

'But it killed him at twenty-one.' The words hung in the air like smoke. 'And there's only one reasonable explanation. Thanks to the gift, he saw something ahead for him which would have been intolerable.'

'I — I guess so. But what?'

'I think you told me, didn't you? Something you heard from his friend Magda. The prospect of endless years of fear, of expecting that one day he would sense a crisis coming which he was powerless to prevent.'

'And he preferred not to be doomed by others,' Sheklov said. 'He chose to make his own decision about an end.'

'But he left a precious legacy,' Bratcheslavsky said. He twisted around on his cushions and picked up a pile of shiny thick white cards, which he held out to Sheklov. Distracted, the younger man took them and turned them over.

They were a set of the pictures from the far-distant reaches of space, which he had so crudely copied for Danty to examine, and which he had so brilliantly and rapidly understood although scores, hundreds of experts had struggled vainly with them for years.

He said, 'The ship has gone, hasn't it?'

'You mean arrived,' Bratcheslavsky said with a sour grin.

'Yes. . .'

Automatically, Sheklov was shuffling the pictures into the reverse of the standard order, meantime visualizing himself, a few minutes from now, consciously imitating what Danty had done with those rough sketches in a roadside restaurant.

Born at the wrong end of time. . .

Oh, what could be wrong with this sick species, mankind, that it had taken Danty with his special, his improbable talent to see the plain and obvious truth? Deformed by fear and suspicion, everybody's mind but his had read threats into these pictures! (He re-heard himself saying to Turpin, the morning of his arrival in the States, 'New York may well be wiped off the map with a total-conversion reaction!')

But the sign of the alien ship was reversed. Whay lay under his hand was the story of the evolution of man — not a threat that he would be driven back to the caves, but a promise that he would travel to the stars! He turned the pictures up one by one, like tarot cards: the caveman with his stone axe; the discovery of fire; that baffling plain disc, which now he realised was symbolic of the invention of the wheel, *not* the Earth wrapped in smoke and fallout; the release of nuclear power; the rocket, the first crude spaceship; the view of Earth as the astronauts and cosmonauts saw it when they made their earliest voyages; the far-distant view of the sun from the orbit of Pluto; the contact made with the unthinkable, incredible, inconceivable ship from the far side of the four-dimensional curve of the cosmos, where matter was anti-matter and time's arrow faced the other way. . . and last of all that wonderful sight which some man might one day contemplate: the whole galaxy, turning like a whirlpool of stars.

Might?

Would. That was the most astonishing thing of all. It might take centuries to work out the philosophical implications of the last conclusion to be drawn from this inverted exponential curve of achievement, but for the time being he at least, Vassily Sheklov, was content to accept it with the force of a poetic or religious truth.

We're going to make it.

Because this alien species could not have learned what — as the pictures proved — they knew about mankind from this meeting: the naked form of a primitive man, above all, waving a flint axe. It followed that they, in their past, had already grown familiar with human beings, in what was still the latter's future. This encounter, the first for man, was for the aliens the last.

No use. It turned his brain topsy-turvy to try and think about it. Leave it to the genius speculators, leave it to the philosophers and cosmogonists and metaphysicians. Right now, the problem was to try and convey some of his sense of certainty to people that Bratcheslavsky had dismissed as 'merely efficient'. How wonderful to know that the human race was not after all going to be destroyed because aliens triggered its own horrible armoury of murder— and how terrifying to know that it rested on his shoulders to convince the world. . .

For a brief instant he felt he knew exactly why Danty

had chosen to destroy himself. And then there was a knock at the door, and someone was standing there, and the someone was saying, 'The First Secretary and the Chinese Ambassador are waiting to receive you, so if you will come with me. . .'